M000076918

This Christmas

The Happy Holidays Series, Volume 2

Michele Brouder

Published by Michele Brouder, 2017.

This is a work of fiction. Names, characters, places and incidents are either a product of the author's imagination or are used fictitiously, and any resemblance to actual persons, living or dead, events, or locales is entirely coincidental.

Editing by Jessica Peirce

Book Cover Design by Rebecca Ruger

This Christmas

Copyright © 2017 Michele Brouder

All Rights Reserved. No part of this book may be reproduced or transmitted in any form or by any means, electronic or mechanical, including photocopying, recording, or by any information storage and retrieval system, without permission in writing from the author.

To God be the Glory

For my father, Henry Zimmer,

who sets the good example

CHAPTER ONE

November 2007

"Geezer!" The familiar voice rang out over the deafening noise of the house party.

Jeff rolled his eyes, plastered on his 'be nice' smile and turned around.

"Hey, Ron, what's up?" Jeff noticed Ron wasn't alone, but then he never was. He wore girls on his arm the way Jeff wore a watch. Jeff darted a look at the girl. She didn't seem to be Ron's type—brunette instead of blonde, short instead of tall. Ron must be off his game, or maybe, just maybe, he was expanding his horizons. Jeff glanced again and was struck by the girl's vibrant green eyes. She gave him a shy smile. Shy? Definitely not Ron's type.

"Holly, this is Geezer," Ron intoned. "We're on the varsity wrestling team together."

"It's Jeff," he corrected.

"How come they call you Geezer?" the girl asked.

Jeff reddened. Ron had been kind enough to give him that tag their freshman year of college. He shrugged.

Ron, however, decided to enlighten her. "Because he acts like an old man. And it takes him forever to do something, especially when it comes to making a decision!" Ron was on a roll. "Any day now, he'll be wearing his pants up around his chest." Ron laughed but the girl looked uncomfortable.

Jeff ground his teeth. Graduation day couldn't come fast enough. Four years of Ron Jensen had been plenty enough. He understood why girls were attracted to him: he was tall, blond and built. But all those winning qualities came to a screeching halt as soon as he opened his mouth. Next to the word 'uncouth' in the dictionary should be Ron's picture.

"Stay here, I'll get the drinks," Ron told his date. "You're safe with Jeff. He's afraid of me."

"I am *not* afraid of you," Jeff protested, but it fell on deaf ears as Ron disappeared into the smoky throng. An ultraviolet light cast a bluish-purplish hue across the room, especially the white t-shirts favored by the wrestlers. The music—some indie band with a forgettable name—played loudly, the bass line adding an underlying thump to the room.

"So...Holly, right? How do you know Ron?" Jeff asked, his curiosity getting the better of him.

"We've been going out for two months." She smiled and her features softened. Feminine. "We have a class together and he asked for some help with a project."

I bet he did, Jeff thought.

He tried not to look surprised. Two months with the same girl? That had to be some kind of personal record for Ron.

"Opposites attract, I guess," she offered brightly.

"What? Like you're a girl and he's a guy?" Jeff teased.

She laughed and tucked a stray curl behind her ear. "No, like we complement each other."

"Give me an example," he pressed. He was dying to hear her take on Ron.

"Well, like he's more social and I'm more of a homebody. All this—" She swept a hand through the air to indicate the crowds of people in the room. "...Really isn't my thing," she said. "Kinda weird, huh?"

"Not at all," he protested. "I understand completely."

"Then there's the fact that he likes to cook and I'm hopeless in the kitchen."

"Really?"

She nodded. "It has to do with having no interest."

Jeff laughed aloud. "Why cook when there's always a perfectly good restaurant or take-out close by?"

"Exactly!" She grinned.

"So are you in your last year, Jeff?" she asked.

"Uh-huh," he said, taking a swig of beer from his plastic cup. "You?"

She shook her head. "No, next year. What's your major?"

"History."

"What a cool field to study! Your classes must be so interesting. What do you plan to do with your degree?" she asked.

"I haven't figured that out yet, sadly. But thank you for not asking if I plan on teaching. That seems to be the default question everyone asks."

"So it's not an option for you, then?"

"No, I don't like kids," he said.

She laughed but then pulled up short. "Oh—"

"I'm joking," he said. Someone bumped into him from behind and he lurched forward, knocking Holly off balance. He quickly reached for her arm to steady her and prevent her from falling. Her skin was soft and warm, and it was with some reluctance that he took his hand away. "Sorry about that," he said.

"No problem." She smiled. "So anyway, you were talking about your plans after graduation."

"Oh. Right. Well, anything other than teaching, I guess. What about you?"

"Teaching," she said with a confident smile.

Jeff cringed, waiting for the big hand of the Lord to give him a good thump on the back of the head for being such an idiot.

Holly continued in good humor, seeming not to have taken offense. "I'm going on for my masters' degree. I hope to teach any grade between kindergarten and fifth. Hopefully, I'll own my own home and have my student loans paid off by the time I'm thirty."

He was intrigued. This girl had her whole life mapped out and he bet somewhere there was a graph and a grid, different colored markers and a secret addiction to stationary supplies. He didn't know what he was having for breakfast the next day, let alone what he was going to be doing for the next eight years. She had managed to sum up her life plan in three sentences. Amazing!

"And the husband, two-point-four kids, two-car garage?" he added, grinning.

She laughed. He liked the way her eyes lit up. "That would be a bonus."

He took another swig of his beer. "Do you get a refund if your plan doesn't work out?"

She looked at him blankly. "Why wouldn't it work out?"

He shrugged. "Oh, I don't know. Life, maybe."

She frowned as if she hadn't considered any deviation from the plan, but then she brightened and lifted her chin and announced, "I am in control of my own destiny."

"If you say so," he said. He admired her confidence; it was an attractive quality.

"I wonder what's taking Ron so long," Holly wondered out loud, glancing around, her eyes scanning the crowd.

"I'm sure he's around here somewhere," Jeff assured her, working to keep the disappointment out of his voice. Why was it that any interesting girl he met was always with someone else? He didn't share with her that he figured Ron was probably sequestered upstairs in one of the bedrooms with a girl that had caught his eye.

"So, Holly," Jeff started in an attempt to straddle the sudden silence. "Tesla or Einstein?"

"Oh, definitely Tesla," she said enthusiastically. "I read the other day that—"

"Hey guys," Ron said as he reappeared at Holly's side. He draped an arm across her shoulders.

"There you are! But where are the drinks?" Holly asked.

Ron shrugged. "Oh yeah, I couldn't get near the bar."

Holly looked skeptical. Ron reached across to Jeff and slapped his abdomen. "What happened, Geezer? The freshman fifteen is going to turn into the freshman fifty soon! I see you're 'wrestling' with that. Get it?"

"Ron!" Holly said, clearly appalled.

"What? We're teammates. We rib each other all the time. He doesn't mind."

Before Jeff could speak, Ron started pulling Holly away. "Let's get out of here, babe. See you around, Geezer."

Holly looked back, gave Jeff a warm smile and said, "Bye, Jeff, it was nice meeting you."

Jeff watched as the incredible girl with the beautiful eyes and the name that reminded him of Christmas was dragged off by the biggest jerk he'd ever known.

He should have just stayed home and watched the hockey game. He finished his beer, left the plastic cup on a table and made for the exit.

CHAPTER TWO

November 2017

Holly Fulbright pulled open the oven door to place the pie shells on the shelf to bake. She frowned when she felt no heat emanating from it. Tentatively, she placed her hand inside but she still felt no warmth. She touched the rack, and it was cold. She peered up at the dial on the old mechanical stove to make sure she had set it properly, turning it off and then back on again. No noise indicating it was firing up. Nothing. She groaned.

This can't be happening! She looked over at the unbaked pie shells and then at the clock. It was almost eight o'clock at night. It had been a long day in the classroom. The kids were so excited going into the Thanksgiving weekend, it had been nearly impossible for them to focus. Holly was expected to bring dessert to her parents' house tomorrow and she was sure she'd never hear the end of it from her father if she showed up empty-handed.

She looked around her new place, one side of a spacious duplex with brand-new carpets and a fresh coat of paint. She'd immediately been taken with it when that nice Mrs. Kowalek had showed it to her. She'd assured Holly it would be fine to bring her cat, Fernando, and—much to Holly's relief—had waved off the idea of a credit check, insisting it wasn't necessary. When she'd suggested a move-in date that was a week earlier than the first of the month, Holly had been ready to sign on the dotted line. She'd finally be able to get out of that dump she'd been renting for the past two years and get away from that jerk of a landlord. But looking at the dark, cold oven, she wondered if it had all been too good to be true.

Technically, it was Mr. Kowalek who was the landlord, or so it said on the lease, but she had yet to meet him. He'd been out of town on work-related training when she'd come to view the place. She'd been there less than a week and it was only late last night she'd seen the dark blue pickup truck pull into the driveway of the adjoining unit.

Irritated, she pulled on her hat and gloves and threw on her coat. A cold front had moved in early over Bluff Falls, New York. Holly felt the weather matched her mood: chilly.

She didn't care how late it was, it was time to meet the landlord.

***

"Ma, don't worry about it, it'll be fine," Jeff said into the phone.

"But I've added too much sage and the stuffing is going to be a disaster tomorrow."

He rolled his eyes. "Somehow, I doubt that." In thirty plus years he had never had a bad meal at his mother's table.

"I'm going to throw it out," she announced with finality.

Jeff panicked. "Do *not* throw it out! At least wait until I taste it." You couldn't have a Thanksgiving turkey without stuffing. It was un-American. It was like eating peanut butter and jelly without the jelly.

"All right, fine, I'll wait," she said.

His doorbell rang. Trixie, his yellow lab, raised her head from her position on the couch, decided it didn't need attention, sighed, and lowered her head back down.

"Ma, I gotta go. Someone's at the door."

"Okay, I'll see you tomorrow."

Almost before the sound of the doorbell had faded, it was followed by a series of urgent knocks.

"Coming!" Jeff shouted. He padded to the front door. Through the frosted glass windowpane, he saw the outline of a short figure. He couldn't imagine who it could be. He hoped it wasn't Mrs. Peters from across the street.

He flipped on the outside light and opened the door. A blast of frigid air hit him in the face. He was glad he had decided to stay in tonight. He was also glad it wasn't his rotation to work. This was a night to cozy up on the couch in sweatpants and a sweatshirt with a pizza and the hockey game. Too damn cold to be out fighting fires.

"Hey, are you—oh! I know you. Are *you* Jeff Kowalek?" Dark curls escaped from under the knitted hat of the petite brunette. Her cheeks and nose were reddened by the weather. Her green eyes, wide with surprise, shone underneath the porch light.

Jeff blinked once. Twice. It couldn't be. It was that girl, Holly, the one from the college party all those years ago. He thought his eyes were playing tricks on him.

"That's me. Wow, yeah, we met a long time ago. You're Holly, right?" He tried to sound casual, but the truth was, he had never forgotten her.

"I am. Holly Fulbright. And I'm also your new tenant, if you can believe it. I just moved in next door last weekend," she answered.

His new tenant! He knew his mother had let out the other unit while he'd been away but he hadn't even looked at the lease or cashed the check yet.

She put her hands on her hips and stared at him. "Well, I hate to start off on a bad note, but the oven isn't working. And I'm only finding this out now when I have to use it."

"Really? Let me take a look at it," he offered. He hadn't a clue about fixing ovens or any major appliances for that matter but he could at least make an effort. It seemed like the thing to do. He quickly pulled on his boots and jacket.

He followed her to her side of the duplex, a little dumbstruck by the unexpected reunion.

She opened the door and he followed her inside. Her space was laid out identically to his: an open floor plan on the main level with a kitchen, dining area, and living room, plus a half bathroom and utility room. There was a connecting garage and upstairs were three bedrooms and a bathroom.

"How's everything else going? Are you settling in all right?" he asked, looking around. The place was sparsely furnished and there were a couple of unpacked boxes stacked in the corner.

"Fine until now. Your wife was kind enough to let me move in early," she said. She blew a breath through pursed lips. She pulled her hat off, distracted.

"My wife?" he asked. He started to laugh. "No, no, she's not my wife. She's my mother."

She reddened. "Sorry. I thought there was a bit of an age difference."

Just a bit, he thought. What did it say about him that she thought his kooky-looking mother was his wife? He didn't want to dwell on that too much. It'd give him indigestion and ruin the perfectly good pizza he was planning on eating later.

Jeff turned the oven on, but nothing happened. He opened the door and looked inside. He had no idea what he was looking for. He went to the utility room and checked the fuse box. He came back in and tried one of the burners on the stove. All the while, Holly watched him with her arms folded across her chest.

He stared at the non-working oven, rubbed his chin and said, "You know, the last tenant mentioned a problem but said he'd try and fix it himself. He never said anything after that so I just assumed he'd managed to repair it." He looked over at his new tenant, who remained expressionless. He attempted some humor. "I guess he fixed it right into the ground."

She didn't even crack a smile. "What did your previous tenant do about cooking?"

"Let's just say Lloyd was a Meals on Wheels type of guy," Jeff said, thinking of the phlegmatic old fella who'd been his tenant from the time Jeff had purchased the duplex five years ago until his death in the local hospice unit over the summer. "Look, I'll replace the oven over the weekend." There was bound to a Black Friday sale where he could pick up a decent oven for a reasonable price.

"That doesn't help me now," she said shrilly, nodding her head toward the unbaked pie shells on the countertop. "I'm in charge of pies for dinner tomorrow."

She looked as if she was about to lose her composure. The last thing Jeff Kowalek wanted to be was a landlord who made his tenants cry. "Hey, no problem. You can use my oven. Problem solved," he said. He saw her posture relax slightly.

"That would be a help but I'd need to use it twice. It's lemon meringue pies I'm making. I need to bake the shells and then the meringue later on."

"That's okay. If it's late, I'll just leave my front door open."

He could see her wrestling with something in her mind. She finally spoke. "Would you be around in the morning? I could bake the meringue then. It would only take fifteen minutes."

"I'm usually up by eight. But I have to be at my mother's house for dinner at two."

"Okay," she said. "Thank you. That works for me." She moved to the counter and picked up a pie pan in each hand.

"Whoa, here, let me help you." He reached out and she hesitated before handing him one of the pie shells. "Come on, let's go."

Holly followed him into his side of the duplex. She gave a little shriek when Trixie lifted her head off the couch to study the visitor. The dog decided it wasn't worth checking out and resumed her resting position.

"Oh, you have a dog," she said, taking a step back.

Jeff glanced at the dog and said forlornly, "Technically, yes. But in reality, no. She doesn't really do much except eat and sleep. She's more like a throw pillow for the sofa."

She eyed the dog warily. "She's a big girl. She doesn't bite?"

Jeff laughed. "Nope. That would require way too much effort."

She seemed to accept his answer. "Look, I really appreciate this. You'd think I'd have noticed by now that the oven doesn't work, but I don't normally cook."

"It seems to me you said something like that when we met at that college party all those years ago. Do you remember that? You were there with Ron Jensen."

"Oh, boy. Ron Jensen. Yes, I remember. Did you know he broke up with me a few days before Christmas that year?"

Jeff had heard that, and in fact Ron had bragged at the time that he hadn't wanted to buy her a Christmas gift as it would only give her 'permanent' ideas. But Jeff would never repeat something that hurtful. "If you ask me, I'd say you made a lucky escape."

There was an awkward silence. Jeff looked at the oven and then back to Holly. "So what do I need to set the oven to?"

"Um, four hundred degrees is good," she said. Her eyes darted around nervously.

Jeff hadn't remembered her as being so edgy or guarded. At the time, she'd struck him as being bubbly, confident. He couldn't help but wonder what had happened in the last ten years.

He clapped his hands together. "Should we put them in?"

She shook her head. "Not yet. It needs ten minutes to warm up."

Silence descended again. "So why lemon meringue?" Jeff asked. "What about pumpkin?"

She frowned. "Pumpkin? Yuck! No one in my family eats it. It tastes awful."

"Not if you put enough whipped cream on it," he said.

She raised her eyebrows. "Not convinced."

They regarded each other nervously, unsure of what to say.

"I think we can put these in now," she said, opening the oven door. Jeff didn't think ten minutes had passed but he wasn't going to argue. She seemed skittish.

"Do you have a pair of oven mitts?"

"Oven mitts? Um, no," he said, scratching the back of his neck. "Will a kitchen towel do?"

She nodded and he handed her a towel from a hook inside the cabinet door underneath the sink. She pulled out the rack, popped the pies in the oven, and looked around. "Probably don't have a timer, do you?"

He shook his head.

"No problem, I'll just use my phone." She went through the motions of setting her alarm. "I'll be back in about twenty minutes."

She turned toward the door.

"Um, hey, do you want to stay and have a beer?" he asked.

"No thanks," she answered. "I've got a few things to do. But I'll be back for the pies."

Before he could say anything, she slipped out the door.

He watched the door close behind her and reached over to give his dog a scratch. "Wow, Trixie, she's not the girl I remember from ten years ago."

***

Holly called Jeff the following morning. She had to search through her paperwork for his number. She still couldn't believe it was him from that party all those years ago. By all appearances, he was doing well. She cringed as she remembered their conversation years earlier and her declaration of having a plan for her life. She must have sounded so arrogant and self-important.

She surveyed her new surroundings, loving the smell of the new carpet and fresh paint and thinking it was a great improvement from the last place, where the landlord had been a jerk. She was glad to be out of there. There were just a few boxes left to unpack. There hadn't been much because there hadn't been much left of her previous life.

"I was wondering if you've ever made meringue," she asked when Jeff answered his phone, trying to disguise the panic in her voice. It was important to her that these pies come out perfect. No mistakes. There had been plenty of those in the past. These pies—an attempt to step out of her comfort zone—were symbolic of her rebuilding her life. But again, she hadn't paid attention. Hadn't looked at the details too closely or done the proper research. That lack of detail had burned her in the past. There was no way she was calling her mother. Then her father would know and she'd never hear the end of it. No, she was going to nail this, even if it took all day.

"Meringue?" he asked. She didn't miss the uncertainty in his voice and her heart sank. What did she expect? The man didn't even own oven mitts. But she was desperate.

"You know, the white stuff on top of the lemon meringue pies?" she explained.

He laughed. "Oh, the four inches of pure sugar?"

"That's it! I've made three batches this morning but they're not turning out. And I don't know what I'm doing wrong. My peaks won't form." She closed her eyes, hoping she wasn't coming across as whiny.

"Well we can't have that—non-forming peaks," he said. "I may know someone who does. Let me call you back."

Holly thought it was ironic how life worked out. She still remembered how appalled she'd been at Ron's behavior at that long-ago party. At the time, Jeff had been nice to her and he hadn't deserved Ron's treatment.

Ten minutes later, there was a knock at her front door.

She opened it and Jeff stepped inside. "Man, it's freezing out there." She looked at him expectantly.

He unfolded a piece of paper from his hand. "I called my mother. She gave me some tips." He handed her the page and her brows furrowed as she tried to decipher his writing.

She handed it back. "I'm sorry, I can't read it."

"No, I'm sorry. Mrs. Cruickshank said I'd never win any penmanship awards. Turns out she was right," He scanned the list. "She said first use a stainless-steel bowl. Make sure your beaters are clean. Not wet or anything. Also, when separating the egg whites from the yolks, do not get any bit of yolk into the whites or the meringue won't stiffen."

"I don't have a stainless-steel bowl," Holly said, looking at the ceramic bowl on the counter still filled with her most recent attempt at meringue. She brightened. "But I do have stainless-steel pots!" She bent down and pulled a two-quart saucepan from a cupboard. It was shiny and brand new and never used. And it had brothers and sisters with it in the cabinet.

"For someone who doesn't cook, why do you have a full set of pots?"

"It seemed like the appropriate thing to have in a kitchen."

She put the ceramic bowl in the sink and began assembling another round of ingredients. "Would you like some coffee?"

"Sure, if it's not too much trouble," he said.

She indicated the coffee maker with the full carafe. "Not at all. Sit down."

She poured him a mug and set it in front of him. "Milk and sugar?"

"Black is fine," he said. "So, what have you been up to these last ten years?"

"Well, I've been teaching third grade over at McGill Elementary for the last seven." She gave him the abbreviated version. He wouldn't want to hear the sordid details of her life. She didn't even want to hear about them. She turned it back to him. "Your major was history, right?"

He smiled. "Yeah, that's right. You've got a good memory."

"And?"

He sipped his coffee. "Took the civil service exam and became a city firefighter. Almost eight years now. I'm over at station nine."

Holly was familiar with it. It was only a few blocks away from her school. Funny, how they'd been so near to each other all these years.

"Are you happy with that?" she asked, reaching for the egg carton.

"It pays the bills," he conceded. He thought about it for a minute. "But yeah, I like it."

She concentrated on gently cracking the eggs, scooping the yolk from one half shell to the other, letting the egg white drop into the pot.

"Whatever happened to Ron?" he asked.

She gave a brittle laugh. "I have no idea. He was such a jerk."

"How did you end up with him, anyway?" Jeff asked. "You didn't seem his type."

She shook her head at her own foolishness. When it came to men, she clearly had a pattern of choosing the wrong ones. "I wasn't. We took a class together: statistics. It was his second time taking it and he needed to pass. He approached me about tutoring him."

Jeff nodded knowingly. "Ah, the old study buddy routine."

"As soon as he passed his final exam—and the class—he dumped me," she explained. It was a long time ago but it still smarted. She had acquired a habit of being made a fool of by men. The only man in her life from now on was going to be Fernando the feline.

"Ron was not known for being a stellar human being," Jeff added.

"I knew he was a player," she said, "But somehow because I wasn't his type, I thought maybe it was different." She added a little cream of tartar to the egg whites. "Instead, I was just a means to an end for him." She turned on the electric handheld mixer, and the noise precluded any comment from Jeff.

She slowly added the sugar, while running the mixer. She felt a combined sense of relief and delight when the mixture began to form into stiff peaks. From the corner of her eye, she studied Jeff sitting at her kitchen table. He hadn't changed that much from college. His hair was a little thinner on top but he still had that solid, compact physique. She tried not to stare at the bulk of his arms beneath his sweatshirt. Probably from lifting and dragging all those fire hoses. There were fine lines crinkled around his eyes. He had aged well, whereas she felt worn down. She knew she needed a vacation but there would be no vacations for years. She took a deep breath. This was no time for negative thoughts. It was Thanksgiving, so she needed to concentrate on things to be grateful for. There was her cat, her third-grade class, her nice new place, and now the meringue, which was finally firming into shape.

Jeff stood and rinsed out his coffee cup in the sink. He peeked into the pot. "Hey, that looks good, doesn't it?"

"It does," she agreed. She spread it over the two pies and dipped the knife, creating peaks and valleys. "I need to put them back in the oven for fifteen to twenty minutes."

"Come on," he said. "I'll take one and you take the other."

CHAPTER THREE

On the way over to his mother's Thanksgiving afternoon, Jeff thought about his new tenant. Maybe he had remembered her wrong. Maybe he had created an idealistic image of her. There was a slight edge to her, a buzz of tension surrounding her that stood in marked contrast to the girl he had met all those years ago. He'd been attracted to her confidence; he remembered thinking at the time that she was someone who could achieve her dreams. He wondered what had happened to derail her from her carefully laid out plans. He supposed that he, too, was different from what she might remember. Or maybe not—he was still alone, after all. That hadn't been a choice, exactly. It seemed more like a default position. There had been one long term relationship but that had ended three years ago. For the most part, he'd been happy with Karen, but her career was everything. When she'd been offered a significant promotion in another city on the west coast, three thousand miles away, she took it without consulting him and had assumed he'd follow her out there. But he couldn't. This was home: Bluff Falls, New York.

He had told Karen he couldn't, he wouldn't, leave his mother. He was her only child. She'd given up everything to raise him all by herself after his father had deserted them when Jeff was three. His mother had never complained; she just got on with it. She'd been a good mother—hell, she was still a good mother, and he was determined to be a good son. So he and Karen put their engagement on hold and tried to manage their relationship via long distance. After one year and an astronomical phone bill, she'd announced that they should go their separate ways. The relationship had run its course, she'd said. There hadn't even been a third party to blame. She had just been through with him. Since then, he'd been a little gun shy about jumping back into the dating game.

He pulled into the driveway of his mother's suburban home. It was a pale yellow cladding-sided ranch with cobalt blue shutters adorning the windows. She had lived there all her adult life. It was the house where Jeff had been raised.

He pulled the bags out of the truck, his contribution to Thanksgiving dinner. There was a six-pack of beer, two bottles of wine, a bottle of whiskey for his mother's boyfriend, Morty, and two boxes of candy, one for his mother and another for Jean, his mother's neighbor.

"Happy Thanksgiving, Ma," he called, coming in through the garage. He put the beer and the wine in the fridge and laid one box of candy on the counter. The kitchen window was steamed up and the air smelled heavenly, like sautéed onions and sage.

His mother, with her hair freshly dyed an impossible shade of red that Jeff knew didn't occur in nature, set the baster down on the counter, closed the oven door and gave her son a hug. "Happy Thanksgiving to you, too, honey," she said. "You're right on time."

"It smells great in here."

"Take your coat off and try that stuffing before I dump it," she said, taking a fork to her carrots on the stove.

Jeff hung his coat in the back hall closet, took the teaspoon from his mother and tasted the bread stuffing thoughtfully. He took another bite. "No, Ma, it's beautiful. If you dump it, I'm going home."

"You don't think there's too much sage?" she asked, her raised, drawn-on eyebrows knitting tightly together.

He shook his head. "Definitely not. What can I do?"

His mother smiled. "Nothing. It's all done."

"Where's Jean?" he asked. As he did, there was a knock on the kitchen door followed by his mother's next-door neighbor coming through with a beautiful pumpkin pie in her hand. Jean had lived next door since Ginger Kowalek had moved there over thirty years ago as a newlywed. Jean had been widowed years ago and had no children. Jeff's mother had whispered to him once that Jean had been run over by a speeding toboggan when she'd been a teenager and somehow that had led to infertility. It seemed dubious to Jeff but then what did he know?

"Hey, Jean," Jeff said. "Let me help you." He relieved her of the pie and set it on the counter. He handed her a box of candy.

Her eyes widened. "Soft centers! My favorite."

Everyone kissed hello. Jean's arrival was soon followed by the appearance of Morty, Ginger's boyfriend. They'd been an item for over ten years, although Ginger had no interest in marrying again after her first husband walked out. Morty was all right. He was good to Ginger and as far as Jeff was concerned, that was all that mattered. Morty chomped on an unlit cigar. He had quit smoking years ago but still needed the cigar. Jeff suspected it was due to some unresolved oral fixation from toddlerhood. Morty handed Ginger a bouquet of flowers in autumn colors, and she put her hand on his shoulder and kissed his cheek. They exchanged a private, knowing look. Morty turned to Jeff and shook his hand heartily, smiling when Jeff handed him the bottle of whiskey.

Ginger shooed the men out of the kitchen and they found themselves in the living room in front of the television. The football game had started.

Morty settled into Ginger's recliner and helped himself to a handful of nuts from a dish on the side table.

"Were you working the night of that three-alarm out on Highway 41?" he asked, looking over at Jeff.

Morty had a police scanner at his house that was on all day and all night. He said it was the reason Ginger wouldn't allow him to move in with her. Jeff suspected it had less to do with the police scanner and more to do with the fact that his mother liked living alone. Morty listened to it like some people watched their favorite TV shows.

Jeff shook his head. "Nah, that was my day off."

"That's too bad. I bet that was a good one," Morty remarked.

Jeff watched the football game, intent. But he knew what was coming next from Morty.

"Almost as good as that propane explosion five years ago."

And we're off, Jeff thought. He sighed, resigning himself to the fact
that he wasn't going to be allowed to watch the game in peace. He
turned to the older man with the shock of enviable thick, gray hair and
said, "But let me tell you about the call we went out on last weekend."

Morty leaned forward, his eyes alight with anticipation, and Jeff
launched into his tale, peppering it with a few embellishments.

Ginger poked her head in from the kitchen. "Oh, Morty, leave him
alone, he doesn't want to talk about work."

"It's okay, Ma, it's nice to have a captive audience," Jeff said.

"To think I spent all those years at the auto plant when I could have
been a firefighter or policeman," Morty said wistfully, leaning back in
the chair when Jeff had finished his story.

***

Ginger set the platter of turkey on the kitchen table and Jeff took the
carving set from the drawer. He began to carve. The table was laden
with dishes: mashed potatoes, green beans with vinegar and bacon,
sweet potato casserole, stuffing, corn, carrots and Brussels sprouts.

"Your mother says you have a new tenant," Jean said, pouring wine
into the glasses set around the table.

"That's right. She's just moved in," Jeff said, carving up the breast.
He had to hand it to his mother. She could cook. The bird was slicing
beautifully and it wasn't the slightest bit dry. He was thinking of all the
turkey sandwiches he'd be eating over the next few days.

"She and Jeff baked pies together this morning," his mother added.

Jean and Morty looked at him curiously.

Jeff stopped carving. "Now wait a minute. Her oven wasn't working
and I let her use mine."

Jean raised her eyebrows. "Really? Already? And she's only just moved in?"

Jeff laid slices of carved turkey on a side plate and began to pass it around.

"Is she married?" Jean asked.

"No."

"Does she have a boyfriend?" she asked.

"I've met her, I got a good feeling about this one," Ginger said to Jean.

Morty looked up to the ceiling, disgusted. "What is it with women trying to fix everyone up? Let the man eat his dinner in peace."

Ginger shrugged. "We're only gathering information."

"No, you're not. You're both trying to poke your noses in somewhere they don't belong," Morty pointed out. He looked to Jeff. "They can't help themselves, you know. It's like a skill set with the female members of our species."

"I'd like to poke something somewhere it doesn't belong," Jean said, eyeing Morty.

They all burst out laughing.

"Anyway, like I said, she's a nice girl," Ginger said. "I rented the unit to her while Jeff was away at a conference."

"Mother knows best," Jean said knowingly with a wink. Morty rolled his eyes.

***

Holly took a deep breath and walked up the drive to her parents' suburban sprawl. With her purse slung over her right shoulder, she balanced a lemon meringue pie in each hand. Once at the back door, she had a dilemma: her hands full, she was unable to turn the doorknob to let herself in. Turning her body gently, wary of the snow and ice covering the porch step, she pressed the doorbell with her elbow.

Soon, she heard the heavy tread of her father's footsteps.

The door flew open and her father stood there.

"Happy Thanksgiving, Dad," she said. "Can you take one of these?" She handed him a pie before he could respond.

He looked at it. "Lemon meringue. I haven't had that in years. Where did you get them?"

"I baked them," she said.

"You baked? Wonders never cease," he said. "Well, I have something to be thankful for today."

She followed him down the hallway into the open plan kitchen and family room. Her mother stood at the stove with an apron on. There was a pot or pan on every burner and through the oven window, Holly could see the twenty-pound turkey browning nicely. A smile broke out on Gloria Fulbright's face when she saw her youngest daughter. She noticed the pies. "Did you bake them?" When Holly nodded, she smiled. "Well, I already know what my favorite part of the dinner will be today." She relieved her daughter of the pie, set it on the counter and pulled her into an embrace. "Happy Thanksgiving, Holly."

Holly looked around. "Is Emma here yet?"

Her father rolled his eyes. "Are you kidding? She likes to wait until the last minute."

"Alan! She's got two kids under the age of six. She's busy. When she gets here, she gets here."

Holly offered to help but her mother appeared to have everything under control in the kitchen. She decided to set the table in the dining room. She removed silverware and wine glasses from the china cabinet and laid places for seven. When she arrived back in the kitchen she heard the sound of car doors slamming outside.

"It sounds like Emma is here," her mother said.

Alan Fulbright looked at his watch as his oldest daughter, Emma, pushed through the doorway with two young children and a harried-looking husband in tow. "Well, that's got to be some kind of personal record for Emma. She's arrived before the turkey's out of the oven."

Emma ignored him and reached up to kiss his cheek. "Happy Thanksgiving, Dad! Mom, where do you want the ambrosia salad?"

"We're almost ready to eat so just put it on the dining room table," Gloria said.

Alan shook his son-in-law's hand. "Richard, how's business?"

Richard, affable as ever and a favorite of Holly's, smiled and said, "I can't complain."

Holly helped Sarah and Emily out of their matching red coats with the black velvet collars. Holly couldn't help but smile at the two of them. They were so lovely.

"Hello girls," Gloria said, kissing each one of them. "Don't you look pretty!" Standing up, she said to her older daughter, "Emma, those coats are adorable!"

Alan Fulbright bent down and held his arms out. "How are my girls?" Holly's nieces rushed into their grandfather's arms with delighted squeals. The girls adored him and vice versa, and this never failed to amaze Holly.

Suddenly feeling overwhelmed, Holly slipped out of the chaos of the kitchen. It seemed too loud and she felt a headache looming. She retreated to the den, with its leather recliners and paneled ceiling. She closed the door behind her and sat down.

Okay, just breathe, in and out. Concentrate on breathing, she told herself. She closed her eyes, trying to regain her equilibrium. *In a couple of hours, you'll be home, and that'll be the first of two major holidays over with.* She opened her eyes when the noise level increased from the kitchen and she saw the door to the den open and watched as Emma entered the room.

"You found me." Holly studied her older sister as she approached. Despite the fact that their personal lives were poles apart, they were close. Emma was a no-nonsense type of person. She carried two glasses of red wine. She plopped down in the recliner next to Holly and handed her a glass.

"Happy Thanksgiving," she said and they clinked their glasses.

They were both quiet, each lost in her own thoughts.

"How are you doing?" Emma asked softly, searching her sister's face.

Holly managed to control the tremor in her voice. "I'm okay. Just waiting for this day to be over with."

"Have you reconsidered accepting some financial assistance from Mom and Dad?" Emma asked.

Holly shook her head. "No, my mind is made up. This is my problem and I'll fix it myself."

"They only want to help," Emma pleaded.

"No way," Holly said firmly. "Besides, I don't want to give Dad any control over my life." She took a sip of wine and stared off into the distance. "Such that it is," she mumbled.

Emma took a sip from her glass and leaned over the arm of the chair toward her younger sister. "I don't think they'd be that bad. Well, Mom wouldn't be."

Holly snorted. "No, but Dad would. I'd never hear the end of it from him."

"That's not true."

"Yes, it is. It's been over two years since that whole mess with Tim, and Dad still goes on about it. If I hear him ask me one more time about how could I have taken my eye off the ball, I'm probably going to throw up," Holly said, setting her wine glass down. She put her head in her hands, defeated. "He goes on and on about how I could have been so stupid."

"You know how Dad is, he tends to react..." Emma pointed out.

"Overreact is more like it," Holly clarified.

"It's only because he cares," Emma said softly. "His heart is in the right place."

Holly remained silent.

"Anyway," Emma continued. "Dad aside, things are moving in the right direction. You figured it would take you five years to sort things out, and two years are down. Let's celebrate that." She raised her glass in a toast.

Holly half-heartedly reached for her own glass and raised it in response. "I'll be too old to care by the time it's over." She let out a big sigh. "I just can't wait for the holidays to be over. December twenty-sixth can't come fast enough." Even though Christmas was a month away, she dreaded it. How could she be cheerful and jolly when her life was in ruins? Plus, the expense of it all...

"Oh, Holly, don't say that. You used to love Christmas."

"I've recovered," Holly said bluntly. "Life has a way of curing you of any foolish, sentimental notions."

Her sister looked thoughtful. "That's too bad, because sometimes that's all you have."

Both sisters were quiet, pensive.

"If you want, I can have Christmas dinner at my house this year," her sister offered.

Holly shook her head. "No, no. That's not fair." Holly and Emma had alternated having Christmas dinner as their mother always handled Thanksgiving and Easter. Holly had hosted twice in the past in her own home. She didn't cook of course, but she had hired a caterer and there had been lots of holiday decorations and music. Emma's young girls and their awe and excitement over the arrival of Santa Claus were always the highlight. "Thanks for offering, though."

The door opened abruptly, startling Holly. She jumped in her chair.

Her father frowned. "Why are you so jumpy today?" When no answer was forthcoming, he announced, "Thanksgiving dinner is on the table."

Emma reached over and squeezed her sister's hand. "Come on, let's go eat."

They stood up to leave and Emma turned to Holly. "Before I forget, Sarah has been bugging me about coming over to your house to bake Christmas cookies."

Despite everything, this made Holly chuckle. "Well, she did bring it up to me back in July. And I did promise her."

"If it's too much, we can put it off until next year."

Holly was a lot of things but she wasn't a Scrooge. The last thing she wanted to do was rain on a little girl's parade. "No, I want them both to come over. You know what? Once my oven's fixed we'll find a weekend night when I don't have to work in the morning and they can come for a sleepover."

Her sister looked concerned. "That might be too much, Holly."

"No, I insist."

***

Holly climbed gratefully into her bed later that night. She couldn't remember ever feeling so exhausted after a Thanksgiving dinner. And it had nothing to do with the turkey. Dressed in a sweatshirt, pajama bottoms, and socks, she burrowed under the blankets. Her cat curled up on the empty pillow next to her, a safe, remote distance away. Through the bedroom window, the streetlamp out front illuminated big, fat snowflakes falling listlessly to the ground. She squeezed her eyes shut. How had it all ended up like this? If someone had told her ten years ago that this would be her life, she wouldn't have believed it. Nothing had gone according to plan.

She'd declined her mother's invitation to join her for Black Friday shopping. She rolled over onto her back, opened her eyes and stared at the ceiling. How was she going to afford Christmas? If only she could wake up and have it be January first. If only. The room was still and the only sound was the soft purr of her cat on the other side of the bed. *Well*, she thought ironically, *at least the cat's content.*

She hoped next Christmas would be different. But somehow, she doubted it.

CHAPTER FOUR

The bright morning sunlight filtered through the slats of the blinds into Holly's bedroom and caught her square in the eye. She groaned and rolled over, reaching blindly for the bedside alarm clock. After a few unproductive grabs, she nailed it and opened one eye to look at it. Nine. Even though she was off from school, she needed to get out of bed. There was a stack of papers for her to grade this weekend and it would be nice to get some of them out of the way today. From outside the window, she could hear muffled voices. Who was outside this early? Were they already recovered from Thanksgiving? Didn't these people have anything better to do?

Begrudgingly, she pulled back the blankets and swung her feet out, feeling around for her slippers. She glanced at the foot of the bed, satisfied to see Fernando curled up with his eyes half open.

"Good morning," Holly said.

The cat regarded her with his usual disinterest.

She padded toward the front window and opened the blinds, squinting as the sunshine filled the room. She noticed Mrs. Peters wrapping Christmas garland around her porch across the way. The dark green artificial pine with the bright red bows looked cheery. She watched as Jeff emerged from Mrs. Peters' garage carrying an aluminium ladder over his shoulder. Jeff leaned the ladder against the porch roof and nimbly scaled it. Mrs. Peters removed Christmas lights from a box on the porch and handed them to Jeff, who started fixing them to her gutter.

"Ugh, Christmas." Holly frowned, stepping away from the window. "January can't come fast enough."

She made her way downstairs in search of coffee. One thing was for sure: there would be no lights or garlands here. She glanced around the interior of her home. Inside or out.

I am so not feeling it this year, she thought. She remembered how as a young girl, she would make a red and green chain using construction paper, removing a link each day as it got closer to the holiday. Ha! Maybe she would make one this year leading up to the twenty-sixth and she could count the days until Christmas was over. Then she thought of her sister's girls. How would it be for them to come over and not find one decoration? She supposed she'd have to put up something. She sighed and poured water into the coffee maker. She scooped coffee into the filter and put the basket in place. She pressed the start button and leaned against the counter, finding comfort in the gurgles and burps the machine began to make.

***

Holly sat at her kitchen table, the book reports from her third-grade class stacked up in front of her. She'd only got through a few of them before the doorbell rang, interrupting her, and she glanced at the clock, frowning.

She padded to the door and answered it. "Hi, Jeff."

"Hey, I'm just heading out to the appliance store to pick up a new stove for you. I was wondering if you'd like to go with me to choose one you like," he said. "Especially since you're the one who has to use it."

Her eyes strayed toward her pile of papers. "No, thanks. I'm not all that particular—whatever you choose will be fine." Besides, the last place she wanted to be was the mall or any shop on Black Friday.

"Oh, okay," he said, sounding a little disappointed.

"But thanks anyway," she added hurriedly.

"I'll let you know when delivery is."

"That's great, you can just text me."

She watched as he retreated down the porch steps and climbed into his truck. She closed the door against the winter chill. She leaned against it, wondering why on earth he would care what type of stove she wanted. She was only the tenant.

***

"Come on, let's go, Trix," Jeff said Saturday morning from the doorway of his bedroom, jangling his car keys. Trixie lifted her head from her place of comfort on the bed and regarded Jeff mildly.

"Trixie, come on, I've got to go to work." Jeff sighed. He looked at his watch, calculating the time it would take to get her off the bed and then get to the station. He looked up to the ceiling and muttered. "Don't be uncooperative. Honest to God, there's a conspiracy going on." He looked at the dog and said firmly, "Outside, now." When she still didn't respond, he boomed, "Let's go!"

The dog slowly stood up on top of the bed and gave a languid stretch. She gave the air a sniff and gingerly climbed down to the floor. She took another look around and gave the air another sniff. Irritated, Jeff rolled his eyes. "Just take your time, why don't you? I'm in no rush, I'm only going to WORK!"

The dog lumbered out toward the back door and the yard. Jeff held open the storm door. The dog paused and tentatively put a paw down on the top step, withdrew it and lowered her head again to sniff it.

"It's a step, Trixie. It's made of concrete. It's the same step that was there yesterday. In fact, it's been there every day of the four years you've been living here."

The dog ran rapidly down the steps, did her business, keeping an eye on Jeff the entire time, and then ran quickly back into the house as if she had only so much time before he locked her outside.

"Unbelievable," Jeff said to her. "You're a dog. You're supposed to love it outside. Only I could end up with a dog who's an agoraphobic."

***

"Miss Fulbright?" a voice rose from the din of the breakfast crowd.

Holly was halfway through the Saturday morning shift at the Olympic restaurant. She had picked up this extra job months ago to cover the basics. Her main salary was dedicated to her fixed expenses as well as that nasty little court-ordered repayment plan.

Holly turned around to come face to face with one of her students, Brianna Hopkins, and her family. Mom, Dad, the kids and the grandparents. The whole damn family. Holly's face fell. She watched as Mrs. Hopkins took in the sight of her: the brown polyester uniform and the tray she held that was laden with plates of eggs and pancakes. No one at McGill Elementary—not even her colleagues— knew that she had picked up an extra job waitressing a few times a week. The Olympic was fifteen miles from her home and her teaching job. She had chosen it because of the distance; she figured she'd never run into anybody there.

The whole Hopkins family stared at her.

"Hey, Brianna," she said with a forced brightness she certainly did not feel. Inside, she was dying.

"Miss Fulbright, what are you doing here?" Mrs. Hopkins asked. Mrs. Hopkins was a hover parent. Not only did she try to control every aspect of her daughter's life but those in her daughter's orbit, as well. Regularly she tried to influence what was going on in Holly's classroom. A woman who barely reached five feet, she wore her hair in a blunt cut, angled so it appeared longer in the front and shorter in the back. She was a woman who took no prisoners.

Holly would have thought the answer was obvious and didn't require any explanation. She shrugged. Brianna's father leaned over to the grandparents and said, "Miss Fulbright is Brianna's teacher over at McGill."

Both grandparents looked at her, unable to hide their surprise. Some days, Holly felt she, too, was unable to hide her own surprise.

"I thought public school teachers were paid well," the grandfather remarked. Holly did not miss the grandmother elbowing him. She didn't feel the need to explain that this job paid for groceries and gas. Lucky for her, she was a light eater.

Holly laughed nervously. "You know, Christmas coming and all that." No need to mention she had been working there since May.

"Oh, right," Mrs. Hopkins said. Holly began to squirm under her unrelenting gaze. Holly could practically see all the calculations, mental, mathematical and otherwise, going on in Mrs. Hopkins' head. She was pretty heavily involved at the school.

Holly's shoulders sagged. By Monday morning, all staff, students, and parents would know that Holly was moonlighting as a waitress at the Olympic on the opposite side of the city. She shuddered as she envisioned a parade of students and their families starting to frequent the restaurant like she was an animal in the zoo.

"Well, enjoy your breakfast," Holly said, indicating toward the tray she held. Luckily, the Hopkins family wasn't seated in her section. She felt thankful for small favors. She gave a forced cheery smile and headed toward her table to deliver the food.

She could never remember being more anxious to punch out. The crowd that morning never let up and bled right into the lunch crowd. Her feet were killing her and her legs ached. She cashed out and headed toward the break room to retrieve her coat and purse.

Sylvia called out from the office.

"Holly, come here to me for a moment," she said in her thick Greek accent.

Holly stepped inside the little inner office. Sylvia, short and wide, and Teddy, tall and lean, had operated the Olympic for over thirty years.

"Would you be interested in working some extra days over the Christmas vacation?" she asked, looking up from her desk, which was piled with papers and ledgers.

Interested wasn't exactly the right word. Holly had been looking forward to some time off, but she was in no position to refuse. She nodded tiredly. Holly would happily have volunteered to work a double shift on Christmas Day, but the Olympic was a 'family' restaurant and remained closed two days a year: Thanksgiving and Christmas.

"Just a couple of days." Sylvia smiled.

"No problem."

The older woman peered at her over the top of her glasses. Not too much got by eagle-eyed Sylvia.

"You look tired, Holly," she stated. It was not a question.

Holly gave a hollow laugh. "No more than usual."

"You've lost weight, too," Sylvia remarked.

"Doesn't every woman want to be thin?" joked Holly, but it didn't come out sounding funny.

"Go to the kitchen and have Teddy give you a bowl of that nice avgolemono soup he made. Chicken and rice."

Holly shook her head. "Oh, no thank you. I just couldn't."

Sylvia sighed, not liking being refused. "You need to take better care of yourself."

"Okay, will do," Holly said, and she slipped out the door before Sylvia could say any more.

***

Jeff hung his coat in his locker at work. He sat down on the bench dressed in a navy t-shirt with the Bluff Falls city logo on the left side of his chest and a pair of navy pants. He looked at his wristwatch.

Kenny called out to him. "Hey Jeff, how was your Thanksgiving?"

Jeff looked over. "It was real nice. How about yours?" His mother had sent him home with enough leftovers of turkey, stuffing and mashed potatoes, not to mention pie, that he was all set for the weekend.

Kenny nodded. He'd started the same time Jeff had and they'd gone through training together. They'd become friends and usually spent their time off watching football, hockey or baseball games. "It was good. You know my mother. Turkey and pasta."

Jeff laughed. "I do know your mother. How is she?"

Kenny's mother was Italian-American. Every holiday included a serving of some form of pasta.

"She's fine. She still wants to fix you up."

Jeff held up his hand and laughed. "I think once was enough, don't you?"

Kenny chuckled. "So, she had a little bit of facial hair, so what?"

"A little bit of facial hair?" Jeff repeated, pausing what he was doing to look at his friend. "I thought I was out with Fu Manchu."

"But seriously, Jeff, apparently she's got a friend whose daughter is coming out of a nasty divorce."

Jeff grimaced. "What am I supposed to do? Hold her hand?"

"Just say yes so I can get my mother off my back."

"If these girls are so nice, why doesn't your mother ever fix them up with you?"

Kenny shook his head. "My mother said she'd never subject me willingly on another female."

They burst out laughing and headed out to the common room. Martha McHenry, the only female firefighter on their rotation, was in the process of making coffee.

"Let's hope it's quiet," she said. "I've got a hangover that won't quit."

"Thanksgiving weekend?" Jeff asked. "You might as well just sit in the pumper all day."

"Shut up, Kowalek," she said good-naturedly. She handed each of them an envelope. "Here are your tickets to the charity dinner."

The annual fireman's spaghetti dinner was usually held the Sunday before Christmas. The cost of the ticket was fifty dollars per person or eighty dollars for a couple. There was also some kind of fundraising activity to go along with it. It wasn't just for firefighters but for the community, as well. The proceeds that were raised went to a different charity each year. Last year, they'd gone to the burn unit at the hospital.

Jeff groaned. "You are a mean woman, McHenry."

She smiled. "I try. The captain told me to pass them on to you. Said he expects everyone to be there this year." She looked pointedly at Jeff.

He scanned the date on the tickets, feeling the familiar anxiety set in at the thought of having to be in a social situation. "I think I have a previous engagement that night."

Kenny laughed. "Sure you do. It's a long-standing invitation with your TV and that thing you call a dog. Yeah, you probably won't be able to get out of that."

"Anyway, the captain said we all have to go. Big charitable event," Martha said. "You don't have anything against charity, do you, Jeff?"

"Of course not," Jeff muttered, wondering how he could extricate himself from this. This would not only involve wearing a suit and tie but bringing a date. And he wasn't going alone. Kenny would suggest they go stag. But how pathetic would that be? That'd be okay if it was senior prom and you were trying to make a statement, but in your thirties?

"Hey, we can go stag," Kenny said, right on cue. Both Jeff and Martha rolled their eyes.

"We are not going stag," Jeff announced.

"Okay, we'll get dates," Kenny said.

"Whoa, slow down there," Jeff said, feeling a sense of panic envelop him. Martha shook her head. Before the conversation could continue down this slippery slope, Jeff took off toward the bay, where the trucks were. It was time to do equipment checks.

***

Holly arrived at work early Monday morning. She put her packed lunch in the fridge in the teacher's lounge. She still had some time before she made her way down to her classroom so she poured herself some coffee from the pot. There were only two other teachers in the room: Terry Stetz, the first-grade teacher, and Robin Morris, the kindergarten teacher.

"How was your Thanksgiving?" Holly asked.

"Beautiful," Robin smiled. There wasn't one hair out of place in her blonde ponytail. "Yours?"

"Nice," Holly answered.

"I ate too much. Glad it's over," Terry grumbled. "Now we've got to get through Christmas." She rolled her eyes. "I hate it. Everything starts too early. And the kids are wild until it's over. They can't focus on their schoolwork." She shook her head in disgust.

Holly stared at her colleague. Terry was in her forties and either single or possibly divorced. There was never any mention of a boyfriend or partner. But you could always count on Terry for a cynical comment.

Robin piped up. "I love Christmas. It's a great time of year."

Terry looked at Robin if she had just grown a second head. "Not me. Counting the days until it's over." Holly thought she and Terry were singing from the same hymn sheet.

Robin pored over her tablet. "Just looking for some more crafts for the kids to do. Today, I'm going to cover the classroom door with a big Christmas tree made out of construction paper and the kids are going to make different ornaments with their pictures and their names on them to decorate the tree," she explained. "Oh, what do you think about this idea?" She showed them a picture of a Christmas-light craft using fingerprints as bulbs.

Holly envied Robin her enthusiasm and energy. She had once felt like that but it seemed like a lifetime ago.

"What are you going to do as a class project?" she asked Holly.

"I haven't decided yet," Holly said. The truth was, she hadn't given it any thought.

Robin looked surprised. "Don't let it go too long. It will be Christmas before you know it."

That much was true.

Terry spoke up. "I was thinking of baking some kind of treat and adding black food coloring. Voila! Christmas coal."

They both looked at her. Robin had a horrified expression on her face.

"Oh, lighten up, I was only joking."

Holly thought she sounded a little mean. So now, as if she didn't have enough going on, she had to come up with an idea for the class craft project. The last three years, her class had done painted Mason jars. The first year, it had been a cute idea. The second and third year, with everything going on in Holly's personal life, it had been a fallback position. She wondered if she could get away with it for another year. Somehow, she doubted it.

The door to the lounge opened and the school secretary popped her head in.

"Oh, there you are, Holly," she said. "Mrs. Hopkins is looking for you."

Holly's shoulders sagged. The last thing she wanted to deal with first thing Monday morning was Mrs. Hopkins.

"Oh, lucky you," Terry said. "I had that nut job all over my back when Brianna was in first grade. Finally, I had to threaten her with a restraining order to get her to back off." She shook her head at the memory of it. "Don't let her trample all over you, Holly."

Holly hoped it wouldn't come to that but she filed it away as an option.

Robin spoke up. "Holly, what I did was give Mrs. Hopkins a project. She wants to be involved in the classroom, so give her something to do. It worked for me. She was happy and she left me alone, and then I was happy."

That sounded a little more reasonable than filing a restraining order.

Holly sighed. "I better get a move on and see what she wants." She stood up from the table and gathered her things, smiled goodbye to her colleagues and hurried out the door. As soon as she exited the room, she was intercepted by Mrs. Hopkins.

"Miss Fulbright, I was just on my way to see you," Mrs. Hopkins called out.

Holly hoped she wouldn't mention anything about seeing her at the restaurant the other day. Holly looked around the noisy hallway, crowded with children winding their way through the corridors to their classrooms before the first bell.

"We don't have much time, the bell is about to ring," Holly said. She wanted to point out that Mrs. Hopkins should really refer to the school handbook, especially the part about making an appointment to chat with your child's teacher. But somehow, Holly knew that suggestion would probably go over this parent's head.

"I wanted to talk to you about exercise balls," Mrs. Hopkins started.

Holly stopped in the middle of the hallway, shifting her bags from one hand to the other. "Exercise balls?" She had a strange idea of where this was going.

"I just read an article about using exercise balls instead of chairs to help kids focus better, especially those kids who need to move around a bit more."

"I may have seen an article on that, as well," Holly conceded. She started moving again toward her classroom. It was almost in sight.

Mrs. Hopkins brightened. "Great, we're on the same page!"

This was how Mrs. Hopkins was dangerous—she knew how to twist words. "I would be willing to purchase and donate enough exercise balls for everyone in the classroom," she said excitedly.

A vision of thirty exercise balls of varying colors bouncing around her classroom flooded Holly's mind. "Well, it isn't that easy. First, I'd need to take a look at all the literature out there and then I'd need to get approval—"

Mrs. Hopkins interrupted her. "Who do you need approval from? I'll go talk to them right now."

Holly hesitated and said, "Look, Mrs. Hopkins, I really appreciate your ideas on how to improve my classroom, but if you would just leave it with me—"

"When can we meet up to discuss it? At the end of the week? Next Monday?" Mrs. Hopkins grilled her.

Holly had arrived at her classroom door. Kids sailed right between her and Mrs. Hopkins in an effort to park their coats and backpacks and get to their desks.

"Let me look at my calendar and I'll get back to you."

"I hold you to it," Mrs. Hopkins said, and she turned on her heel and disappeared into the throng of grammar school children.

Holly blew out a breath, wondering if she'd ever get Mrs. Hopkins off her back.

CHAPTER FIVE

"Okay, Stan, thanks, I got them," Jeff said into his phone. His widowed neighbor across the street had slipped pizza coupons into his mailbox, like he did every Monday morning after he'd read the Sunday newspaper.

Only a couple of minutes later, Stan appeared at Jeff's front door. "Come on in, Stan. What can I do for you?" he asked.

"When I called, I forgot to ask you if you had any vacuum cleaner bags," the old man replied, stepping in and stomping his feet on the mat, dislodging chunks of snow.

"Somewhere around here," Jeff said. "They'll be for a canister, though, not an upright. Is that what you need?"

"Canister, that's the one." Stan said, pulling off his cap and smoothing back his thick white hair. His face was faded tan from the time he spent outdoors in the summer tending his garden and his beloved tomato plants. A hearing aid was visible in his left ear. Stan Bauman had been the first person Jeff had met on the street when he bought the duplex five years ago. He was a good neighbor. His wife, Ida, had already been dead many years from cancer by the time Jeff met him, but Stan still reminisced about her fondly from time to time.

Stan looked to Trixie, who lounged on the couch.

"She's a nice dog and all, Jeff, but I think you've got a lemon there," Stan remarked. He went over and rubbed the dog's head. The dog groaned, closed her eyes and rolled over onto her back. Stan laughed. "I'm not rubbing your belly, old girl."

"Speaking of old girls, how's the dating scene going?" Jeff asked. Although Stan missed his late wife, he was also a serial dater.

"Taking Gladys to the movies tonight," he said. "They're showing *It's a Wonderful Life* down at the community center."

Jeff smiled. "Smooth. Gladys? She's new."

"Met her at the supermarket," Stan said casually.

Jeff shook his head. "I have never met anyone who has managed to pick up as many women as you do at the grocery store. What's up with that? Is it the way you push your cart? Is it how you bag your groceries—putting the eggs on top? Because they seem to fling themselves at you as soon as you walk in."

Stan smiled and said nonchalantly, "What can I say?"

"How do you do it? What's your secret?"

"Well, weekday mornings are the best. You won't find my age group there after dark. Also, I have a secret weapon."

"I'm dying to hear it," Jeff prompted, noting the irony of getting dating advice from an octogenarian.

"Sympathy."

"Sympathy?" Jeff repeated, unsure if he'd heard correctly.

"It works every time," Stan explained. "Women can't stand to see suffering and if you can get them to feel sorry for you, you're in."

Jeff thought about his present circumstances: a slightly overweight man with a possible case of social anxiety disorder. Although his mother would protest and say 'husky' and 'shy.' The women should have been lining up at the door.

"C'mon, what's your line?" Jeff asked.

"Produce aisle. I'll stand at the tomatoes a little too long and when someone appealing comes over, I'll say, 'Which ones would you recommend? I just lost my wife and this shopping thing is new to me.'"

"You dog! Ida's been gone for years!"

Stan shrugged, grinning. "They don't know that. Besides, I've gotten some great tips on how to check whether melons or avocados are ripe enough. You should try it."

Shaking his head, Jeff chuckled. Somehow, he couldn't picture himself handling fruit and asking for a date. "I don't think it'd work for me."

"How do you know until you try? Some girl would be lucky to have you," Stan said.

"Thanks, Buddy, but I'm fine on my own," Jeff said unconvincingly.

"No, you're not. I see you over here, all locked up and never going out. You should be out with people your own age, not holed up in your house. You're never going to meet anyone in your living room."

Jeff flushed, embarrassed to be called out on his life, or lack thereof. He nodded toward the couch. "Right now, Trixie is all the woman I can handle."

Stan tut-tutted. "She's half-dead, but I'm not giving up hope on you yet, Kowalek."

"Well, I appreciate that."

***

"Hey, how's it going?" Tina asked, carrying in two full canvas grocery bags.

Holly maneuvered around the bags and gave her friend a hug. "Welcome to my new abode!"

Tina set the groceries down on the countertop in the kitchen and took a look around. "Wow, it's nice. Everything is so clean and new-looking." Tina Dupree had been Holly's friend since high school. There were no secrets with her; she knew everything going on in Holly's life. It was refreshing to be with her as Holly didn't have to put on appearances for appearance's sake.

"It is," Holly agreed. "It's so much nicer than the last place."

"Don't remind me. That nitwit of a landlord." Tina made a face and mimicked Holly's former landlord. "'Don't park in the driveway,' 'Make sure the storm windows are down in the winter,' 'No running the dishwasher or wash machine after eight pm.' Ugh! I don't know how you stood it."

"Luckily, I don't have to stand him any longer. So glad to be out of there."

Tina began emptying the grocery bag. "I know you don't like cooking, so I brought you some premade meals." She pulled out cartons of gourmet food and loaded them into the refrigerator.

Holly picked one up. "Hmm. Beef bordelaise. Really, Tina, you didn't have to do this."

"I know, but I wanted to," Tina smiled. "Think of it as a house-warming gift."

If it were anyone else, Holly would have felt embarrassed but there was no need to with Tina. No scorecard was kept. It was just an easy friendship. Tina pulled out some fresh fruit from the canvas bag. "Some raspberries and blueberries, because I know they're your favorites."

She loaded them into the refrigerator, as well. She shut it and removed the last two items from their bag. "And most importantly, wine and chocolate." She smiled at Holly and asked, "Corkscrew and glasses?"

Holly nodded toward the cabinet. "I'll get the corkscrew, you get the glasses."

After opening the bottle and letting it breathe for a few minutes, the two friends settled in at the kitchen table with their drinks. "So tell me about your neighbors—who lives in the unit next to yours?" Tina asked.

Holly sipped her wine, rolling it around in her mouth. "It's my landlord, actually. His name is Jeff. Funny thing is I met him once, years ago in college."

Tina arched an eyebrow and gave her a sly smile. "Oh, I see."

Holly laughed and shook her head. "It wasn't like that. I was with Ron at the time."

Tina stuck out her tongue. "Yuck."

Holly opened the box of chocolate and studied the legend on the inside before choosing a soft caramel.

"Well, come on," Tina prompted.

"Come on, what?" Holly asked.

"You know, is he married? Is he dating anyone? Is he datable?"

Tina loved opportunity in any way, shape or form. Whether it was a BOGO deal at the supermarket or a single man who presented possibilities, she was all over it like green on grass.

Holly shrugged. "He's really nice." She paused and looked around. She felt funny talking about Jeff like this.

"Nice? That's it? My grandmother is nice. What's wrong with him?" Tina asked, suspicious. "Lazy eye? A humped back? Looks at your boobs instead of your eyes when he's talking to you?"

Holly burst out laughing. "No, he's cute."

"Cute? Is that the best you can do?" Tina admonished. "Puppies and kittens are cute, Holly."

Holly considered. "He has nice eyes. Soft. He's not real tall. Not thin, but not fat. Solid, I guess you'd say. Pretty good biceps, too—he's a firefighter for the city."

Tina's eyes widened. "Oooh, I like that. Call him over here. He can practice the fireman's lift on us."

Holly laughed. "Shut up. He's a nice guy."

"Will he be Mr. March in the annual calendar?" Tina asked.

Holly shook her head. She didn't think Jeff would be into that. He seemed kind of shy. She'd only been living there a few weeks, but other than work, he didn't really seem to go out that much.

"But do you think he's attractive?" Tina pushed.

Holly poured more wine into their glasses. She'd thought so back in college, but now? She hadn't given it much thought. She had enough on her mind already. Holly squirmed, uncomfortable at being put on the spot. "Yeah, Tina, I guess he is."

Tina brought her glass to her lips, raising her eyebrows. "I might just have you fix me up with him."

***

"Now, Jeff, you didn't forget that I won't be here next week," his mother said as she set a plate of her famous pot roast in front of him.

Jeff was over for their weekly Tuesday night dinner and he had, in fact, forgotten about that, along with the reason why. "Refresh my memory," he said, picking up his fork and knife. The roasted potatoes and vegetables were just how he liked them: golden and crispy. It was a nice break from eating takeout.

"Morty and I have the informational meeting about our trip to Italy in the spring," Ginger said excitedly.

"Oh, that's right," Jeff answered. His mother and her boyfriend had taken an Italian cooking class at Bluff Falls High School through the continuing adult education program and had never recovered. From there, they'd enrolled in Italian 101 at the local community college and someone from that class had the bright idea that they should all go to Italy together. And who better to lead the group but their instructor. Once that ball started rolling it became a runaway.

"Don't worry about it," he said. "I can come over on Wednesday."

Ginger shook her head. "No, that doesn't work for me either, honey. It's our night to host the bridge group." She cut up her meat, forked a piece and began to chew thoughtfully. "Besides, don't you have better things to do than hang out with your mother?"

Jeff put down his fork and knife and stared at her. "Are you dumping me?"

She giggled. "Of course not, honey. But I don't want you to miss out on any opportunities because you're stuck with me."

"Ma, I am not stuck with you," he said firmly. Sometimes, he wondered about his mother's mindset and where she came up with these crazy ideas.

"Does that Holly have a boyfriend?" his mother asked, trying to sound casual while buttering up a slice of bread.

Jeff laughed. "Why, do you want to ask her out?" He took a generous mouthful of pot roast.

"Oh, Jeff," she scolded, swatting his arm. "You know I don't swing that way."

Jeff almost spit out his food. "'Swing that way?' Where are you learning this stuff? What kind of television are you watching?"

"You know, honey, I've been around the block once or twice in my life," she said.

"I hope you're referring to this neighborhood block you're living on."

"No, I was thinking you should find out for yourself whether she has a boyfriend," Ginger explained. "Does she?"

Jeff's next forkful of food paused midair on the way to his mouth. "Wow, you don't beat around the bush."

"You know I don't." She was trying to look serious but her too-high pencilled-on eyebrows were saying something else.

He hadn't seen any sign of Holly having a boyfriend. However, it was hard to believe there wouldn't be someone in her life. "I'm not sure if she does," he said. "We haven't gotten around to having a heart to heart yet."

"Since you're not coming here for dinner next Tuesday, maybe you might want to ask Holly out for dinner," Ginger said ever so casually, as if she were asking him to pass the salt.

Jeff opted for silence, as he thought it was the best defense. If he said nothing, her idea might just go away of its own accord.

But his mother wouldn't let up. "Have you ever thought about asking her out?"

"No," he lied. The truth was since Holly had moved in, he had thought of little else. But she seemed disinterested. He'd seen the look on her face when he'd asked her to go stove shopping with him. It had bordered on disbelief. Looking back, he couldn't believe it, either. What had possessed him to ask her to go to an appliance store?

"Well, you should think about it," his mother pressed.

Jeff was beginning to lose his appetite, which was a shame because the pot roast was delicious.

"She seems like a nice girl. And you're a nice guy," Ginger said. "And it would be so convenient with her living right next door."

"Yeah, think of all the money I would save on gas," he deadpanned.

"Exactly!" she said. "So? You'll think about it, will you?"

Jeff stared at the ceiling for about a moment and announced, "There, I've thought about it. No."

After dinner, Jeff brought up the plastic totes from the basement that contained all his mother's Christmas decorations. He assembled her artificial tree and untangled three bundles of lights, testing them to make sure they were still working. By the time he left, it was snowing heavily.

***

Jeff's second-floor bedroom overlooked the front of the house and the street, so when he awoke the following morning he only needed to lift his head a few inches off the pillow to see the two feet of snow on the ground outside. He groaned and rolled over, pulling the blankets up over his head. It was just too warm under the covers and too cold outside for him to get up. He settled back in, his head comfortably ensconced in his pillow, and just began to doze off again when he heard the all-too familiar scraping-metal sound. There it was. Once. A second time. He knew what it was and who it was, but he slipped out of his bed, muttering under his breath, to confirm it. Standing at the window in a t-shirt and boxers, he peered out against the blinding morning brightness.

"Oh man," he grumbled when he spotted Stan shoveling his driveway. "I've told him a million times…"

Jeff padded to the dresser and pulled out a pair of clean socks and a sweatshirt and a pair of jeans. Throwing them on, he thought, *I've told him I'd do it, but the man refuses to listen. Why he doesn't hire a snow removal service for the winter is beyond me. He has more money than God.*

When I retire, that's the first expense I'm treating myself to, is snow removal.

He looked over to Trixie, lying inert on the rug, and asked, "Do you want to go outside?" The dog didn't even bother to lift her head. "I didn't think so. Just thought I'd ask." He bent down and patted her on the head. "Just thought you might want to shake it up a bit." He jogged down the stairs and mumbled to himself, "Why I bother is beyond me." At the front door, he slipped into his boots and pulled his coat off the hook, making sure his gloves were in his pocket.

He trotted across the road, calling, "Hey, Stan, what are you doing?"

Stan stopped and leaned against his shovel. "Take a guess." His nose was bright red and his eyes looked a startling shade of blue against the white backdrop. He was wearing a hat with flaps on it and he had a pair of chains over each shoe. It was amazing what you could get away with when you were over eighty years old.

"Okay, smarty," Jeff said.

"Ask a stupid question..."

"Stan, I told you I'd shovel your driveway," Jeff said.

"Sonny, I can shovel my driveway myself. It's good exercise."

"Are you kidding?" Jeff tried to take the shovel, but Stan held it out of his reach. "C'mon, Stan, let me do it. The snow weighs a ton. You'll have a heart attack." And Jeff ought to know. He could no longer count how many calls the fire department had answered for people—mostly men—suffering heart attacks while clearing off their walkways after a big snowfall. It was nothing to mess around with.

"You don't need to do this for me, Jeff," the old man said.

Jeff nodded. "I know that, Stan. It's not a question of me needing to do it. It's me wanting to do it."

Stan looked away and sighed heavily. "Will you have a cup of coffee?"

Jeff smiled. "I'll tell you what. If you let me finish shoveling, I'll drink the whole pot."

Stan smiled and headed back into the house.

Once Stan had disappeared inside, Jeff shook his head, smirking. Stan was a great neighbor; he couldn't risk anything happening to the old guy. He looked at the front of Stan's tidy red-brick home. When he was finished here he'd volunteer to hang the Christmas lights off the gutter like he did every year, and like he'd done for Mrs. Peters.

He bent over, sliding the shovel toward the grass. He lifted, grunting at the weight of it, and flung the snow on the lawn. The packed wet snow was like concrete. He continued clearing Stan's driveway, thinking he'd need to do his own and Holly's, as well. As soon as Christmas was over, he was going to pick up a snowblower in a January sale. Every year, he said he'd buy one in July, but when summer came around, he always forgot. He had just made it to the apron of the driveway when he felt a surge of pain radiate from his chest to his left arm. In a matter of seconds, a crushing pain girdled his chest. Instinctively, he dropped the shovel and clutched his chest. If he could just catch his breath. His peripheral vision narrowed and he began to stagger toward the snow bank. He needed to sit down, and quickly.

CHAPTER SIX

Holly had popped her head outside to check the mailbox before going back upstairs to get dressed for work when she spotted Jeff in Stan's driveway, dropping the shovel to the ground and grabbing his chest. She gasped and ran outside, still in her nightgown and bathrobe, and flew across the street. The chilly air numbed her body but she didn't care.

"Jeff!" she shouted.

When she reached him, he gasped, "Call 9-1-1."

"Come inside," she instructed. She didn't want him sitting on the cold snow.

He shook his head. "Won't make it."

Alarmed, she reached for her cell phone and realized she didn't have it. She ran up Stan's drive, up the porch steps and banged on the door.

Stan opened it with a scowl. "What the—"

She cut him off. "Jeff needs an ambulance. I think he's having a heart attack." Her voice wavered on the last part of the sentence.

The old man went as white as the hair on top of his head. "Jeff?" He peered over Holly's shoulder and caught sight of Jeff sitting on a mound of snow, slightly slumped forward. Without another word, he turned around and sprinted into the interior of his home.

Holly returned to Jeff, who still complained of severe pain. She took his hand in hers and began to massage it. Briefly, he looked up at her and she gave him a reassuring smile. She had taken CPR last year when the staff at the school were offered it, and she was mentally going over the steps in her head, grateful that he was still conscious. When she heard sirens in the distance. Holly exhaled the breath she'd been holding.

Stan emerged from the house, the worry on his face aging him. Suddenly, he didn't seem as spry as Holly initially thought.

"Jeff, that's it. No more shoveling for either one of us!"

She remained at Jeff's side and watched with relief as the ambulance rounded the corner.

"Here they come," she said. She realized she was shaking, and it wasn't from the December cold.

From his seated position, Jeff looked up at her. "Go inside, Holly, you'll freeze to death."

She looked down at her bare feet in her slippers and frowned.

"I'm all right," she fibbed. "How are you feeling?"

"It kind of feels like it's going away," he said.

The ambulance pulled up and Stan waved them over. As the two paramedics jumped out, they gave Holly a brief glance, exchanged looks and turned their attention toward Jeff. Holly pulled her robe closer and crossed her arms over her chest.

"Will you call my mother?" Jeff asked Stan.

The old man nodded. Holly thought he didn't look too well and wondered if he'd need an ambulance himself.

"Try not to worry her too much," Jeff added. He turned toward Holly. "The dog—"

Holly nodded. "Don't worry, I'll take care of her."

"The door's unlocked," he said.

Holly nodded, taking in his ashen face. She was worried about him.

***

Jeff tried to ignore the conversation going on above his hospital bed between his mother, Morty, and Jean. But it was proving to be difficult, and their hovering was increasing his anxiety. They had come early: eight sharp, 'to beat the crowd' Morty had said and to get a good parking spot. Jeff knew visiting hours weren't until later and he wondered how they had gotten around that little house rule. From the emergency room yesterday, Jeff had been admitted to a hospital room late last night for observation. He was waiting for a doctor or nurse, or anyone, really, to come into his room if only to give him a break from the crowd that had gathered at his bedside. He was scared that the chest pain might return. But the three of them were so busy talking they probably wouldn't even notice if he should happen to lose consciousness or something.

Morty inspected Jeff's breakfast tray. The toast was cold and the eggs were rubbery. "How do they expect you to get better with food like that?" he asked no one in particular.

"Hospitals aren't noted for their food," Ginger said, taking a closer look at Jeff's breakfast and scowling. "Is that oatmeal?"

"What you need is someone to love," Jean said. Her smile disappeared and she added, "Someone other than your dog." She began to fuss with the blankets on Jeff's hospital bed, straightening them out. "That's why your heart hurts."

Jeff rolled his eyes at this assertion and Morty countered, "You're watching too many Lifetime movies."

"He needs a wife!" she announced, as if she'd been inspired by the Holy Spirit to jump to this next logical conclusion.

"A wife! Are you nuts?" Morty barked.

"Ssh, you two," Ginger admonished. "What Jeff needs is some rest."

The man in the other bed coughed discreetly from behind the curtain.

Morty made an 'oops' face and lowered his voice. "Sorry, Jeff."

"Don't worry about it, Morty," Jeff said. He squirmed in the bed, uncomfortable at the thought of the three of them discussing his personal life.

"Seriously, kid, you've got to take better care of yourself. It'd be a shame if anything happened to you," Morty observed.

And on that cheery note, Jeff thought to himself.

Jean continued smoothing the blankets at the foot of the bed. "Jeff, to me there's no one better than you," she said. Her eyes filled up. "I don't want to see you end up alone. I'd like to see you settled down with your own family. I know your mother would, too."

"No pressure, Jean," Jeff said half-jokingly.

"You need to get out more. Don't be afraid."

"I'm not afraid," he said, hating that he sounded more defensive than he wanted to. He loved Jean. She'd been like an aunt to him his whole life. And although she liked to give unsolicited advice, she meant well.

She raised her eyebrows. "You're not just a little bit afraid?"

"Nope." He refused to be baited, especially with his mother and Morty standing there and another patient just on the other side of the curtain, most likely listening. So much for confidentiality in hospitals.

She shrugged and sighed. "All right. If you say so."

"Oh, look, Jeff has company," his mother whispered. The four of them looked up to see Holly hesitating in the doorway.

"Well, is she coming in or not?" Morty asked. Ginger elbowed him.

At home, the idea of visiting Jeff in the hospital had seemed like a good one. Holly had called the school saying she'd need to take a sick day, then picked up a bouquet of flowers before making her way over. But now she wasn't so sure. After all, she wasn't family or even a close friend. She was just his tenant. And she hadn't known him that long. She saw Jeff sitting up in the bed by the window, and there were three other people standing at his bedside. All four of them were staring at her. Jeff wore a tentative smile, but the other three were grinning.

"I hope to dear God, you're coming to visit me," said the old fella in the bed by the door, startling Holly. And that decided it; she was going in.

"Sorry." She smiled apologetically at the solitary old man.

"That's the kind of luck I've got," he said, closing his eyes.

Holly took a deep breath and walked over to Jeff's bedside. "Hello," she nodded at the group gathered there. "Jeff, I brought you flowers, I wasn't sure—"

"It's fine, thanks," Jeff said. "Ma—"

"I don't know if you remember me, I'm Jeff's mother," Ginger said, relieving Holly of the flowers.

"Of course I remember you, Mrs. Kowalek," Holly said. Who could forget that hair and those eyebrows? The poor woman looked awfully pale and tired under her make-up.

"Flowers?" Jean smiled, nodding. "How thoughtful."

"Not if you're allergic," Morty said seriously.

Holly looked at Jeff, feeling panicky. "Are you allergic?"

"No, I'm not," Jeff said and he shot Morty a look. He made a quick round of introductions.

"We'll go down and grab a cup of coffee," Ginger said to Jean and Morty, who both nodded.

"Don't leave on my account, please," Holly said.

"You two might want to be alone," Ginger said. "We'll be back." Holly was momentarily mortified at the implication, but the three of them disappeared before she could protest any further.

Jeff squirmed in discomfort. "Sorry about that. They mean well."

"It's all right."

"Sit down," he said with a nod toward the bedside chair. "How are you?"

"I'm fine, but more importantly, how are you?" she asked.

"Well, I'm still alive, which is something, I guess," he said.

"It's a big something, Jeff," she said quietly.

"Hey, I just want to say thanks for helping me out yesterday morning," he said sincerely.

She shrugged. "It was nothing."

"Well it was something. And I really appreciate it."

She smiled at him. "I'm glad I could help."

"How's Trixie?" he asked.

Holly pulled the chair out from the corner and brought it nearer to the bed. She removed her hat and scarf as she sat down. "She's good. Look, I don't mean to pry or anything—"

He looked at her, expectant.

"Is there something wrong with your dog?" she asked, concern on her face.

Holly was pleased when Jeff laughed. "Why, I don't know what you mean," he said.

She grinned. "Well, I'm no expert on dogs, but yours seems a bit, um—"

"Just say it," Jeff prompted.

"Underactive?" she asked.

"Do you think?"

"No, really, though," Holly protested.

"She was a stray. Rescued her from a fire at an abandoned building. She was still a pup. I took her home. She was never really active as a puppy. I took her to the vet and spent thousands of dollars trying to get to the bottom of it."

"Wow, you're devoted," Holly said, eyes widening.

Jeff shrugged. "What can I say? I like dogs."

"And what did you find out? Was it something rare?"

Jeff chuckled. "Oh, it was something rare, all right."

Holly waited.

"It's her personality. She's just lazy. My dog is basically a couch potato. My cousin's dog jumps off piers and catches frisbees in his mouth. Has the ribbons to prove it." He shook his head. "But Trixie? We consider it a good day if she can lift her head off the pillow."

Holly burst out laughing.

Jeff grinned. "Has she even noticed I'm gone?"

Holly thought for a moment. "You know, I think so. She seems a little mopey."

"How can you tell the difference?"

It seemed to Holly that Jeff was making an effort to be upbeat. "Do you know when you'll be able to come home?"

He shook his head. "I'm still waiting for the doctor to come in."

"Was it a heart attack?"

"No, thank God. It was a cardiac event, whatever the hell that is."

"I see." Holly was about to add that she was glad to hear it, but his mother reappeared. She must have inhaled that cup of coffee.

Ginger smiled. "It's very nice of you to visit Jeff."

"I probably should get going," Holly said quietly. She looked briefly back at Jeff.

"Oh, don't leave because of me," Ginger said.

"Thank you, Mrs. Kowalek, but I really should get going." Holly stood up and offered Ginger her chair. She pulled on her hat and scarf.

"Where are Jean and Morty?" Jeff inquired.

"Morty took Jean home. He'll be back for me later."

"Don't worry about Trixie, I'll take good care of her until you get back," Holly said.

"Thanks again, Holly. I really appreciate it. Hopefully, I'll be home soon."

***

After Holly left, Jeff turned to his mother. "What was that all about? Wanting to leave the two of us alone?"

His mother smiled, but Jeff couldn't help but notice the exhaustion on her face. He realized he was the cause of it and figured he should dial down his tone.

She shrugged. "She's a nice girl, Jeff. You could do a lot worse."

"Well, since I'm not doing anything, it doesn't really matter."

"All I'm saying is that she's a nice girl, you're a nice boy—"

"Ma, I'm not eight."

"Okay, you're a nice guy and you should think about it."

"About what?"

"Holly. Dating. Marriage. Kids."

"Wow, don't hold back." He couldn't help but wonder why his mother was so hell-bent on fixing him up with his tenant. He hoped this wasn't going to be the topic of conversation every time he saw her. It was starting to wear him out.

Mercifully, their conversation was interrupted by the appearance of a doctor entering the room. He was tall, ridiculously handsome and somewhat older than Jeff.

"Mr. Kowalek!" boomed the doctor. Ginger jumped in her chair, startled. "I'm Dr. Greene, the cardiologist. You've been referred to me by the emergency room." He extended his hand and Jeff shook it.

Jeff gestured toward his mother. "This is my mother, Mrs. Kowalek."

"Nice to meet you." The cardiologist shook Ginger's hand, as well.

Jeff noticed that the doctor's teeth were blindingly white like a movie star's. Absentmindedly, he ran his tongue over his own teeth. One of his front teeth on the bottom was chipped, courtesy of a flying hockey puck in a street game he'd played in high school.

Dr. Greene set up his laptop on the small counter in the corner and pulled out a stool with wheels and sat down. "So, it was crushing chest pain that brought you in to us."

Jeff nodded.

"How are you feeling now?" the doctor asked, clicking the pad on the laptop.

"Better," Jeff said with uncertainty. He wasn't having the chest pain he'd experienced in Stan's driveway, but still, he was anxious. "Will it happen again?"

"They told us it wasn't a heart attack," Ginger prompted.

The doctor smiled again and Jeff wondered whether they were his own teeth or veneers. "Fortunately, no." Dr. Greene said. "Your cardiac enzymes were negative. Although the initial EKG showed some cardiac changes, the follow up one was normal. Angio normal. Bloodwork was mostly good but your cholesterol was elevated—"

"Too much pizza," Ginger interrupted.

Jeff shot her a look.

The doctor nodded. "So, although it appears you've had nothing more serious than a minor cardiac event, you're going to need to make some lifestyle changes. You're currently twenty pounds overweight—"

"I hope you're not going by those outdated life insurance charts," Jeff joked.

The doctor gave a small chuckle. Jeff thought his attempt at humor was worth more than that.

"Twenty pounds? Oh, Jeff," Ginger admonished from her chair. She hadn't noticed his spare tire until the doctor had pointed it out just now.

"Ma, please," Jeff said through gritted teeth.

The cardiologist continued. "You're not obese, but the bulk of your weight is carried around your midsection, and studies show that extra weight around the abdomen leads to a greater risk of cardiac events or heart attacks. Mr. Kowalek, what line of work are you in?"

"I'm a firefighter," Jeff said.

"I'd imagine you'd have to be in pretty good shape for that job," the doctor said.

"Yes, that's true. I've always passed my annual physicals."

"I'm sure, but your admission here is a game changer. We're going to discharge you later today with a brochure on a heart healthy diet: low sodium, low cholesterol."

Low fun. Jeff closed his eyes and groaned. He saw his pizza-and-beer nights flying out the window.

"Follow up with your own doctor in two weeks."

Jeff nodded.

"Count yourself lucky, Mr. Kowalek. Lots of people don't get second chances," he said. He closed his laptop and stood up to leave the room. "Have a great Christmas, but don't overdo it."

"Yeah, thanks, doc," Jeff said, thinking that if ever there was a time to shoot the messenger, this was it.

Neither Jeff nor his mother said anything for a moment. They were letting what the doctor had said sink in. Jeff couldn't help but feel a little depressed.

Ginger spoke first. "That's it, Jeff. No more pineapple upside down cake. No more Watergate cake. No more macaroni and cheese."

"Okay, Ma," he said.

"No more slush cake, no more Texas sheet cake—"

"Okay, Ma, I get it," Jeff said, a little more loudly than he'd intended.

Ginger stood up from her chair, rearranging the strap of her purse over her shoulder. She looked at him seriously. "No, honey, you don't get it. I'm your mother and I'm not going to lose you over a pepperoni pizza."

After she left, Jeff lay back and stared up at the ceiling tiles, trying to figure out what he was going to do with the rest of his life.

CHAPTER SEVEN

Holly stood at the end of the counter at the Olympic, slicing three pieces of mince pie for the ladies at table three. She was fantasizing about the nice hot bath she was going to soak her aching body in once she got home. Hearing a whistle, she tilted her head to one side and frowned. She tried to distinguish it from the other noises of the restaurant: hushed conversations, the gruff voices coming from the grill line and the clattering of dishes. Once the slices were plated, she returned the pie pan to the glass carousel, which housed a variety of homemade desserts. Her tips had been good that day and she thought she might just treat herself and take home a piece of that chocolate cream pie. As she closed the case, she heard it again, a loud, commanding whistle. Quickly, she looked up to the patrons of the diner and noticed that all conversation had stopped, and attention had shifted to the raised hand of the man at table four in her section. He made eye contact with her as if to say 'Yeah, you.'

Holly's cheeks burned. She wished the floor would open up so she could fall in. Hurriedly, she hoisted the tray of desserts on her arm and returned to her regulars at table three, setting a piece of pie in front of each of the ladies.

"Can I get anyone more coffee?" she asked with forced brightness.

The woman with her back to the whistler said, "No honey, you better see what he wants before he starts whistling Dixie."

Holly nodded and stepped over to the adjacent table, where two middle-aged men sat with their coffees.

The shorter, balding one indicated his nearly-empty cup. "Didn't you hear me whistling?" he demanded.

"Oh, I heard you all right," Holly said, indignant. "In fact, the whole restaurant heard you. But the thing is, whistles are for dogs and I am not a dog."

He was speechless. Holly headed toward the waitress station and grabbed the coffee pot off the burner. She returned to the table and was met with silence. She refilled both their cups. She suddenly felt weary, as if all the fight had gone out of her. Resigned, she said, "My name is Holly if you need anything else."

After they departed, Holly cleared their table to find a five-dollar tip for the two cups of coffee. She bit her lip. It was a gesture on the part of the customer, but to her it meant that her humiliation had a price tag of five dollars. She was in no position to refuse it. Principles came at a price she couldn't afford. She swallowed her pride and shoved the bill into her uniform pocket. She couldn't wait for her shift to be over.

After she'd clocked out, she walked briskly to her car at the back of the parking lot, ignoring her throbbing legs and aching back. She didn't know how the other waitresses did it. She had such respect for them. For her, this was a temporary gig until she was in a better place financially, but for some of the girls here, this was all they had. On their feet all day, subject to all kinds of abuse from customers if the food wasn't right, even though they hadn't even cooked it, just delivered it to the tables. Earning less than minimum wage because of the tips. Inside her car, Holly laid her head down on the cold steering wheel and began to sob. Three more years of this. She wasn't sure how she was going to manage. After a bit, she lifted her head and wiped her eyes. She turned the key in the ignition and headed for home.

***

Jeff had been home for a few days when he decided to venture out to the grocery store. His mother had prepared some meals for him so he wouldn't have to order take-out. But now, he was beginning to suffer from cabin fever and shopping was a good excuse to get out of the house. Besides, he was hungry. His initial impulse had been to order a pizza but he caught himself. There was no way he wanted to feel that crushing chest pain again. He looked through his cupboards and his refrigerator and was immediately discouraged. There were only the basics. There was a can of soup but it had expired two years ago. He groaned.

He grabbed his coat off the hook and keys off the hall table. He'd make a run to the grocery store and stock up on some healthy foods.

While in the hospital, he had had time to think. A lot of time, lying in the bed staring out the window, watching the snow fall as the calendar ticked off the days to Christmas. At first, he'd been scared, but then he'd recognized the experience for what it truly was: a wake-up call. He was awake. Hell, he was alert. And he was also grateful. Grateful for the second chance. He didn't want to hide anymore. He didn't want to end up in a documentary about a guy gone missing who was found with his sofa grown around him, unable to be separated from it. He was still young, not even thirty-five yet. He wanted to live. He was going to make the effort. He was going to eat better, live better, and he'd start by taking some small steps. No more take-out, although he'd miss his good friend, pizza. It was time to get acquainted with the produce aisle.

He grabbed a shopping cart out of the corral and wheeled it into the store, whistling a Christmas tune. He bravely passed the selection of holiday goodies, determined to choose appropriately. In the produce aisle, he paused for the first time ever to appreciate the amazing selection and the colors. In the past, he had sailed right on through, pausing only long enough to pick up his standby bunch of bananas. Jeff figured now was as good a time as any to test out Stan's advice. Taking a page right out of the old guy's playbook, he headed for the tomatoes. There were all sorts of varieties to choose from: Beefsteak, tomato on the vine, roma, cherry. As luck would have it, he *was* going to need some help choosing. He studied the price difference and noticed an older woman walk by. She picked up a clear plastic bag, threw in some tomatoes, tossed them into her cart and left. She made it look so easy. Another woman approached and grabbed a bag. She was blonde with pretty blue eyes. Jeff decided to throw caution to the wind.

"Um, excuse me, could you tell me which are the best tomatoes?" he asked. He tried to put on a sad puppy dog face.

She scowled at him. He relaxed his facial muscles a bit. She relaxed in return and shrugged. "I don't know. I always buy the cheapest." And she walked away. Damn!

Undeterred, he walked over to the lettuce selection. There were bags of prewashed mixed varieties as well as heads of iceberg, Boston, Bibb and more. He started to go for the bagged selection as it seemed easier, but an opportunity in the form of a lithe curly-haired woman presented itself. She reached for the hearts of romaine. Jeff saw that as a sign.

He chuckled to get her attention. "Who knew there were so many varieties of lettuce?"

She turned to him and smiled. "I know! Sometimes it's hard to choose."

Jeff would have said that about chicken, cheddar and broccoli pizza versus Greek pizza. Not lettuce. However, encouraged, he plowed on.

"I'm just recovering from a serious cardiac event and I've got to get my act together," he said, putting his head down.

She immediately reached out and touched his arm. "I'm sorry to hear that. How are you feeling now?"

Jeff shrugged. "I'm getting there, thanks." He didn't want to tell her he was actually feeling better, because then there would be nothing for her to feel sorry about.

"Good for you," she said. Her hand remained on his arm and he lifted his face and saw sympathy in her eyes. "Just try to take it one day at a time."

"I am, but it's difficult doing it alone," he said, wondering if he was laying it on too thick.

She removed her hand and began fishing through her purse. She was going to give him her number! He couldn't wait to tell Stan. She pulled out a business card. "Here, take this. My husband and I run a

Bible based weight loss group. We meet every Wednesday night at the parish hall."

To conceal his embarrassment, Jeff nodded his head so fast he was afraid he'd end up with a case of whiplash. "Thanks, thanks, I really appreciate this." He accepted the card from her and shoved it into his pocket. He took a bag of pre-washed lettuce, threw it into the cart and headed toward the fruits, hoping he'd have better luck with the bananas.

"Jeff?"

Jeff turned and came face to face with Holly. This surprised him in a good way.

"You've come home!" she exclaimed.

He was relieved for the distraction. He could put the dating game in the produce aisle to bed for a while.

"I am, ma'am," he said. She looked good. Her pretty dark hair spilled over her shoulders in loose curls and her green eyes blazed.

"How are you feeling?" she asked, concern flooding her face.

"Much better," he said. He drew in a deep breath. "I'd like to make you dinner to thank you for taking care of Trixie while I was in the hospital."

Holly scrunched up her nose. "Oh, Jeff, that's not necessary. She was no trouble at all."

Jeff pressed. "It's the least I can do."

She considered it for a moment. "Do you cook?"

"Well, not really, but I want to learn," he said sheepishly.

She grinned. "All right then."

He glanced at the contents of her cart. There were a few no name brand items: cereal, soup and laundry detergent. There was also one box of Christmas cookies. He picked them up and smiled. "I haven't seen these around since I was a kid." They were a simple shortbread with anise flavoring and red and green sugar sprinkles.

Holly looked at them. "Me neither. I saw them and it reminded me of Christmas when I was a little girl, so I threw them in the cart. Probably stupid."

"I don't think so. Hey, how did Trixie do while I was in the hospital?"

"I didn't want her to be lonely so I took her to my house and she stayed there overnight. I hope you don't mind."

Jeff laughed. "No, not at all. I'm surprised she went."

"Well, it took some coaxing as you can imagine," Holly replied.

Jeff grimaced. "Sadly, I can."

"Once she got there, she was fine. It was just trying to get her off your sofa that was the hard part."

"I know," Jeff agreed. Oh boy, his Trixie was a winner. Only he could get a dog that was less enthusiastic about leaving the house than he was.

"You know, I'm not much of a dog person. We always had Pekingeses growing up but they were nothing more than ankle biters." Holly winced at the memories. "But I can honestly say that Trixie is the first dog I really like. She's my speed."

"Actually, Trixie is no speed," Jeff said.

"Even Fernando warmed to her," Holly mused.

Fernando? "Well, I guess as long as Fernando's happy," Jeff ventured.

"He's used to having me all to himself," she explained.

Jeff frowned, picturing some buff Latin American boyfriend. *I bet*, he thought with some surliness.

"He likes to let me know in no uncertain terms that he's the boss," she said affectionately.

Jeff was beginning to feel uncomfortable with this much detail about Holly's personal life. He looked away.

A silence descended.

"So, you're shopping," she noted, indicating the lone bag of lettuce in his trolley.

He looked sheepish. "Yeah, I've got to cut back on the pizza and the beer. I see you're shopping, too. I thought you didn't cook."

She laughed. "Just because I don't cook doesn't mean I don't eat. I tend to eat a lot of salad—"

"By choice?" Jeff grimaced.

"Yes! I love salad. It can be yummy if you know what to add to it."

"Can you add pizza to it?"

"No," she chided. "C'mon, I'll help you."

He nodded. "Sure, I need all the help I can get."

He watched in amazement as she threw all sorts of things into his cart other than lettuce and tomatoes. There were strawberries and fresh mint, lemons, black olives and feta cheese. There were chickpeas and beets. She threw in a bottle of olive oil and balsamic vinegar.

Jeff raised his eyebrows. "Now what do I do with all this stuff?"

Holly gave him a reassuring smile. "Experiment. For instance, try some romaine with mint, strawberries and balsamic vinegar. Or some spinach with lemon, olive oil, feta and black olives."

He followed her, pushing his cart, over to the peppers. She continued, "But you can't live on salad alone. You'll need to expand. Do you have a grill?"

He nodded. He'd bought a grill three years ago but had only used it once. It had seemed easier to just pick up the phone and order something already hot and ready to eat. He'd never confess this to her.

She was talking but he wasn't listening. He was too intent on watching her as she examined the peppers. There were shades of the old Holly there from all those years ago. Fernando, huh? Too bad. But that was the kind of luck he had.

She bagged up a red and yellow pepper. "Just add some color."

He had to agree with her. He was ready to add some color to his life and he might as well start with his salad.

CHAPTER EIGHT

All that food shopping had made Holly hungry. And when Jeff had asked her one more time at the checkout if she'd let him make dinner for her as a thank you for taking care of his dog, she agreed. It would be nice to share a meal with someone rather than eating alone. She had to admit she enjoyed Jeff's company. He could really be funny at times. Sometimes, it caught her off guard and a laugh would escape, surprising her. She had thought she'd never smile again, let alone laugh. After she had dropped her groceries off, she went over to Jeff's side of the duplex.

He had just finished unloading his own groceries. Trixie lifted her head from the sofa and gave her tail a slight wag at the sight of Holly.

"How are you, Trix?" she asked, patting the dog's head. The gentle motion made the dog sleepy and she settled back into the couch with a contented sigh.

"How's salmon with salad and some wine?" Jeff asked from the kitchen, holding up a bottle of white wine.

Holly nodded. "Sounds good."

"Let me look up how to grill salmon and I'll get right on it," he said.

She joined him in the kitchen and looked over his shoulder as he read information off his phone.

He straightened up and clapped his hands. "Okay, let's pray the grill works on the oven."

"You've never used it?" She asked.

"No, I haven't. I have an actual grill out in the backyard but I haven't used it since I bought it three years ago. Thought it'd be safer if I used the one in here."

"I can make the salad if you'd like," she offered.

"That it be great," he said. "There's a mixing bowl in that cabinet there."

He pulled salad items out of the fridge and laid them on the counter. He turned on the grill of his oven and unwrapped the piece of salmon. He turned to Holly. "Hey, how's your new oven working?"

"To be honest, I haven't used it yet," she said and then quickly added, "But my nieces are coming over soon to help me bake cookies."

Holly assembled a salad with romaine, feta, tomatoes and a few black olives. She tossed it with some fresh squeezed lemon and olive oil and set it on the table.

"Can I set the table?" she asked.

"Sure," he said. "Silverware in that drawer there. Plates and glasses in that cupboard over there."

After the table was set, she sat down and crossed her legs and watched as Jeff finished grilling the salmon. He turned the grill off and plated up the salmon.

He set her dish in front of her with a generous portion of salmon on it. Her stomach growled in response. She served up some salad on each of their plates. He grabbed the wine bottle off the counter and filled their wine glasses.

Jeff held his glass up and said: "To better eating!"

She clinked her glass against his and took a sip. "Tell me a story about working as a firefighter. Answering a call or something."

He looked thoughtful for a moment. "We have this guy who likes to hang out at our firehouse. His name is Vinnie. He must be in his seventies by now. When I first started, he showed up one cold winter night." Jeff paused, fooled with his napkin and smiled at the memory of it. "Anyway, he bangs on the firehouse door late one night and tells us he's got a fire in his kitchen. So, as I'm raising the alarm, I say to him, 'why didn't you call us?' He says, 'my phone is out of order.' I asked, 'why didn't you use your neighbor's phone?' He says he didn't want to bother them because it was so late. He had walked six blocks to the fire station to tell us he had a fire in a frying pan in his kitchen." Jeff shook his head. He looked at Holly. "You know what the kicker was?

He asked us for a ride back to his house because his legs were too tired from the walking. Not to mention it was cold outside."

He put a forkful of salad into his mouth and chewed thoughtfully. "Hey, this is pretty good."

Holly draped her napkin over her lap. "What happened then?"

Jeff sighed. "Well, by the time we got there, the whole kitchen was on fire as well as the entire back section of the house. I think that one eventually turned into a three-alarm." He paused, taking a sip of his wine. "Anyway, since then, Vinnie tends to hang out at our firehouse. Some of the older fellas like to play cards with him."

"What does that mean? A three-alarm? I hear that all the time: it was a three-alarm fire, a four-alarm fire..."

"It's how many consecutive alarms after the initial call. When you first arrive at the scene of the fire, the incident commander determines if more men or more water are needed and then the next alarm is rung. Basically, it's a fire that needs backup."

Holly nodded. "How many firefighters would there be at a four-alarm fire?"

"Roughly a hundred. A five-alarm fire, you're talking up to two hundred firefighters."

"Have you ever been on a five-alarm fire?" she asked.

He nodded, cutting up his salmon with his fork. "Once. It's an experience I don't care to repeat."

She sensed that he didn't want to go into it, so she dropped the subject.

Holly thought he had the warmest eyes she'd seen since forever. They were a deep brown with amber flecks. They were eyes you could get lost in if you were so disposed.

"Are you all ready for Christmas?" Jeff asked, looking up from his meal.

Caught off guard, her face fell. Jeff picked up on it.

"Hey, hey, I'm sorry. It can be a tough time of year for some people. It's not jolly for everybody."

She lowered her gaze, looking at the napkin in her lap. By sheer force of will, she pulled herself together and lifted her head. She tried a smile but wasn't convinced herself. And she could tell Jeff wasn't, either.

"What's going on?" he asked.

She shook her head. In the immediate aftermath, she had told her sister Emma and then gradually she had told Tina. She didn't want to vocalize it. She just couldn't. She didn't want to assign the whole mess any more power than it already had.

Finally, she said, "If you don't mind, I don't want to talk about it. Let's just say it's been a rough couple of years."

Jeff nodded. "I understand completely. I'm in a similar situation. Ever since I hit puberty, it's been rough."

Holly couldn't help but laugh.

"I mean, look at me. I've got a dog at home who doesn't even want to socialize with me," he said.

She felt some tension ease out of her body and she realized that it felt good to laugh. It was a step in the right direction.

***

After dinner and the clean-up, Holly thanked Jeff for dinner and began to put her coat on.

"I'm heading out for a quick walk up and down the street if you want to go with me," Jeff said trying to sound casual. He had enjoyed dinner but more than that, he had enjoyed her company.

"Sure, I'd love to," she said.

It had snowed some more while they had been eating dinner. The snow crunched under their feet as they walked home. The sky was inky black and the air was damp and crisp. Jeff made random observations about various Christmas decorations and lighting as they made their way up the street.

"See, look at that house," he said, pointing across the road to a two-story house that was literally lit up like a Christmas tree. The house and the trees in the front were strung up with lights. There were illuminated snowmen and reindeer on the front lawn. A carousel of Christmas images played across the garage door and red and green floodlights bathed the entire front yard. "Every Christmas Eve, we get a call from them. They're great people but they always manage to set their broiler on fire. Every year. One time while we were there, all the power went out. Overloaded circuit," Jeff shook his head. "But they're really nice. The wife makes the best appetizers."

Holly looked at him, confused.

Jeff explained. "After we put out the fire, they always feed us. In fact, whenever I run into them in town during the year, they always say, 'See you on Christmas Eve!'"

Soon they were back at their own duplex. Jeff wasn't ready to go inside just yet. He leaned down and scooped up some snow. "Good packing snow," he observed. He molded it into a snowball.

"I suppose," she said, unsure.

He shook his head, tossing the snowball from one hand to the other. "No, it is." He tossed the snowball up in the air.

He took two steps back and threw the snowball at her, hitting her on the arm.

"Hey!" she said, surprised. Quickly she grabbed some snow and nailed him in the face, laughing.

Jeff scooped up more snow and yelled, "And I was going easy on you, Fulbright!"

After a few minutes, they stood next to each other on the walkway to the porch, breathless and red-cheeked.

"Do you want to come in for a cup of coffee?" Holly asked.

He looked in the direction of her side of the duplex and Fernando came to mind. As much as he liked Holly, she had a boyfriend and there was no sense in setting himself up for that kind of disappointment.

"I better not," he said quietly.

"Oh, okay," she said. He thought she sounded disappointed and he was sorry for that.

"Another time," he added hastily.

They both watched as Mrs. Peters from across the street marched over to them. She wore a tweed cape over her robust figure with a matching cap, and she held a square white bakery box in her hands.

"Hey, Mrs. Peters," Jeff said. "This is my new tenant, Holly Fulbright."

"I've seen you around, dear," she said, eyeing up both Holly and Jeff. "Well. Isn't this cozy?"

Holly looked mortified. "I was..." her voice trailed off.

"Of course you were, dear," she replied.

"What can I do for you, Mrs. Peters?" Jeff asked trying to spare Holly any further insinuations.

"I've brought something for you," she said indicating the box. "And I wondered if I could speak to you for a minute?" she asked. She looked at Holly as she said to Jeff, "Privately."

Holly got the hint. "I'll talk to you later, Jeff." She disappeared inside before he even had a chance to say goodbye.

∗∗∗

Jeff unlocked his front door, and Mrs. Peters sailed right past him.

He followed her into his kitchen and watched as she set the box down on his kitchen table.

"Stan told me you ended up in the hospital," she said, turning around and putting one hand on her hip. "So, tell me how you are feeling?"

"Much better," he answered.

"Good. We were all worried about you, Jeff," she said seriously.

"That's very kind of you," he said.

"You're the anchor of this neighborhood," she continued. Jeff began to feel uncomfortable. "We'd all be lost without you."

He was starting to feel like he was terminal.

"Thanks, Mrs. Peters, I appreciate that," he said.

"No problem," she smiled. "Anyway, I just wanted to see how you're doing. I've picked up some low cal, low fat cookies."

"How thoughtful." Jeff tried to sound enthusiastic.

"As much as I'd love to, I can't stay. Must get to the mall to finish my Christmas shopping."

He walked her to the door.

Before she left, she turned to him. "There is something I want to talk to you about." She hesitated. "Would you please let me fix you up with my niece, Trudy?" she asked, like she did every time she met up with him.

Jeff was about to give her his standard reply when he paused, thinking about his determination to change things. He smiled and said, "Sure, why not?"

Mrs. Peters was caught off guard and looked momentarily stunned. Her rate of recovery was notable. "Really?"

Jeff laughed. "Yes, really." After all, it was just a date. Not a marriage proposal. "Look, why don't you see if you can fix something up for next week. I'm off Monday or Tuesday."

Mrs. Peters became as excited as a five-year-old on Christmas morning. "I'm on it!" She slipped out the door and practically ran back to her house, her cape flying behind her, her stride one of purpose and determination.

***

The alarm rang through the firehouse in the middle of the night. Automatically, Jeff rolled out of his bed and quickly pulled on his navy t-shirt and pants. He ran toward the fire pole with the rest of the crew. He slid down and headed toward the driver's side of the fire engine where his gear awaited. He pulled on his bunker pants and boots, his mecko hood and turnout coat. The last thing he did before he jumped up into the driver's seat was put his hat on. His chief sat in the front seat next to him, booting up the laptop.

"What've we got?" Jeff asked.

"House fire."

When they turned onto the street in question, they didn't need the house number. From their position, they could see the house ablaze at the far end of the street, the orange flames jumping high against the black midnight sky. By the time Jeff parked the pumper at the curb, he could tell by one look the house would be a total loss. He glanced toward the open garage and saw two cars completely ablaze. There was the sound of hissing as the tires caught fire and then a popping noise as they blew up.

He saw the family of five huddled in the driveway in their pajamas, coughing. Someone shouted, "Is there anyone else in the house? Has everyone gotten out?"

The father, dumbstruck, nodded, still staring at his house going up in flames. The mother sobbed and gasped. There were three blond-haired children, very young, staring at their house, mesmerized. Paramedics wrapped blankets around their shoulders and led them gently away to waiting ambulances. As Jeff unreeled the hose from the truck, he could the hear mother's cries as she was led away by an attendant, her arm around her smallest child. A lump formed in his throat. It was a sound he was familiar with: the sound of anguish. He knew he would never forget it. He looked up and down the street. All the other houses were decorated for Christmas, and this house, the burning house, was the brightest of them all. It was too surreal. Still, he needed to get to work and do his job.

***

The crew had no sooner returned to the firehouse from the house fire when the alarm sounded again. There were collective groans all around. It was six in the morning and still dark outside and although Jeff's shift was due to finish in two hours, they were obligated to answer this call. As the alarm sounded through the firehouse, Jeff grabbed the gear he'd just taken off and pulled it all back on. He hopped back into the driver's seat of the pumper. The big garage doors opened and once his battalion chief was seated beside him and typing the address into the laptop, Jeff rolled out of the firehouse, followed by the ladder truck. There was a call down to the senior citizens' apartments on Smith Street. It was an ugly brown brick building, low-income housing that had been built with government funds. Expense had been spared.

"Someone smoking in bed," Martha said from behind him.

"Smoking in bed? Who does that anymore?" Jeff asked. "It's so 1970's."

"Some old geezer, I guess," Kenny responded.

Jeff flinched at the use of the word 'geezer,' the old nickname he hadn't heard since his college days. He wondered briefly if Holly remembered it. If she did, she hadn't mentioned it.

He pulled the truck into the fire lane and they all jumped out without delay. Paramedics were carrying an old man out on a stretcher. He was huddled in a blanket, coughing a phlegmy cough and wearing an oxygen mask.

From a third-floor window, flames could be seen inside a window, though the glass was still intact. That was a good sign because a broken window meant oxygen feeding a fire.

"Kenny, do a three sixty around the entire perimeter and tell me what I got," the battalion chief ordered. "Murphy, get that hydrant open. Kowalek, get that hose from the pumper attached to the connection."

Jeff located the fire department connection behind some bushes in front of the building. With the help of another fireman, he unreeled the hose from the pumper and hooked it up to the pipe. From there it would supply the apartment building's fire hose on the third floor.

Jeff returned to the pumper and as soon as the command came over the radio to "Charge the line!" he went about the task of filling the hoses with water.

Jeff watched as his commander pointed at two guys. "I want one of you beneath the apartment on the second floor and the other above it on the fourth floor to make sure this fire doesn't spread."

The fire was brought under control in no time. Kenny emerged, removed his helmet and strode over to Jeff.

"We managed to keep it contained to the bedroom. I guess he was a smoker. Ashtrays everywhere. I counted at least ten strategically placed through the kitchen, living room and bedroom." He walked away, shaking his head.

"Shouldn't he be going to the hospital?" Jeff asked Phil, the paramedic.

Phil barely gave him a glance. "He refused."

"That's crazy. He needs to be checked out."

"We've told him all that."

Holding his helmet under his arm, he walked over to the bent figure. "Sir, are you okay?"

"Yeah, yeah, I'm fine," he said. He held an unlit cigarette between his thumb and forefinger. "You wouldn't happen to have a light, would you?" he asked, peering up at Jeff.

"I think you've done enough smoking for today," Jeff said. He looked around, wondering what would happen with this old fella. "Do you have family we can call?"

The old man shook his head. "Nah. No family." He laughed bitterly. "Well, none that would have me." He was in dire need of a shave and a clean t-shirt.

"Do you have someplace to go?" Jeff asked.

"Sure, I do believe the Red Cross are sorting out my future accommodations," he said smartly.

On cue, a woman approached with a Red Cross badge hanging from a lanyard around her neck.

"Mr. Redmond, will you come this way?" They helped him off the curb and Jeff watched as he walked off to his fate.

On the drive back to the firehouse, all Jeff could think of was what Kenny had told him about that man's apartment with the ashtrays everywhere and him sitting on the curb in the cold telling Jeff he had no family to call. In his mind, Jeff replaced the ashtrays with pizza boxes and beer bottles and saw himself in thirty years.

***

Holly was heading toward her classroom when the school's principal, Janet Murakowski, intercepted her. The grim expression on her face worried Holly. She wondered briefly if she was going to be fired but then dismissed the thought as ridiculous, the-sky-is-falling kind of thinking.

"Is everything all right, Janet?" Holly asked.

Janet shook her head. "No, it isn't. I just got off the phone with Patty Sanders' sister."

Holly froze. The Sanders had three children going to McGill. Their only daughter, Grace, was in Holly's class. She was a quiet, shy girl who loved to read. Holly swallowed hard.

"Their house caught fire last night and burned to the ground."

Holly's hand flew to her mouth. "Oh no." Her eyes widened and she reached out and laid her hand on Janet's arm. "Are they all right?" She dreaded the answer.

"Luckily, they are. They are all in the hospital being treated for smoke inhalation but they're all expected to recover. The children will be out from school for a few days."

Holly breathed a sigh of relief. "Oh, thank God everyone is all right."

"The house is gone. They've lost everything. They got out with just the clothes on their backs, and that was pajamas."

"Oh, how awful." She thought of Grace and the way she would proudly show Holly any new book she got. How devastating for all of them, and so close to Christmas.

"I've sent an email to all the teachers in the school but I wanted to talk individually to the teachers who have the Sanders children in their classes. I thought we could have a meeting after school to talk about what we could do. Some kind of fundraiser, maybe, or clothing drive for the children."

"That's a great idea."

Before the bell rang, Holly settled at her desk, trying to prepare for the day, but she couldn't focus as her thoughts were on Grace Sanders and her family. She wracked her brain thinking about ways they could pull together what was obviously going to be much-needed funds, as well as Christmas presents for the Sanders' family. She put her purse in the bottom drawer of her desk and took out her lesson plan. As she reviewed the lessons she planned to teach that day, she realized that for the first time in ages she hadn't been thinking about her own problems. She had more than her fair share of them, but she was an adult and much more adept at handling trauma. Not like the Sanders kids. To be woken up in the middle of the night and pulled from their warm beds and thrown out into the cold, snowy weather... to watch as your family home, a place laden with memories, went up in flames... Holly shuddered at the vision. She glanced over to the row of seats by the window, where Grace normally sat in the third desk. Something would definitely have to be done for the Sanders family.

Her thoughts were interrupted by the bell. Her students poured in and headed toward the back of the class to hang up their coats and backpacks. They were all full of chatter, still wound up from their weekend off. She stood up and cleared her throat. "Alright, boys and girls. I need you to take your seats and stay quiet for a moment."

She watched as everyone slid into their seats. Everyone, that is, except for Jimmy. Jimmy had a short attention span but he was good kid. He remained at the back of the room, digging through his bag.

"Come on, Jimmy, I need you to sit down."

"But I can't find my pencil case," he protested.

"Don't worry about it right now, we'll take care of that in a minute. Right now, I need you to take your seat."

Jimmy looked at her and made his way to his seat.

She came out from behind her desk and stood in front of it, leaning against it.

"Now, class, there's something important I need to tell you and I need you all to listen very carefully."

***

At the end of what had turned into a very long shift, Jeff cleaned his gear, stripped his bedding and stored everything in his locker. He was exhausted. He was going to clock out and go home and crash in his bed. At that moment, he was grateful for his no-maintenance dog. Kenny approached him.

"I'm going to ask one last time, Jeff," Kenny said.

Jeff narrowed his eyes and looked at him.

"Would you please go out with Rosemary? The daughter of my mother's friend?" Kenny pleaded. "Help me get my mother off my back. Just one date. And then never again. I promise. I'll tell my mother you've decided to become a priest or something."

"Yeah, okay, tell your mother to set me up," Jeff said.

Surprise spread across Kenny's face. "Really? You're not joking?"

"Of course not, set me up," Jeff said.

Kenny slapped him on the back. "Thanks, Jeff. I owe you."

***

"Come on, just humor me and come out for one drink," Tina pleaded. "I'm wrecked from all this Christmas shopping and I could use some time out."

"Take your coat off, Tina," Holly suggested.

"No, I'm not taking my coat off, you're going to put your coat on," Tina said, folding her arms across her chest. "Besides, it will do you good."

Holly could not hide her irritation. "Wasting money I can't spare on a couple of drinks? I seriously doubt that will do me any good."

"Okay, here's the thing. You've had a terrible two years. We all agree on that. But you've also withdrawn from life. That's enough of that. It's time to re-join the land of the living."

"I will, I promise, once the holidays are over," Holly said, knowing her friend had the best intentions but also partly wishing she would just leave. She was sorry she'd answered the door. She just wanted to be left alone. Why couldn't anyone understand that?

But Tina wasn't one to take no for an answer. She picked up Holly's coat and held it out for her. "Either you put it on or I'll put it on for you."

"I can't go out looking like this. I'd need to do something with my hair and put some makeup on," Holly protested, trying to buy time.

Without a word, Tina rifled through her purse and pulled out a hairbrush and lip gloss. "Here you go. And like I said, either you do it or I will."

Annoyed, Holly grabbed the brush and pulled it through her hair. She took the lip gloss and looked at it, muttering, "This isn't even a shade I would normally wear."

Tina smiled. "Live a little on the edge."

***

As they walked out of Holly's house, Jeff was exiting his side of the duplex with his friend, Kenny.

"Hey, Hol," Jeff called.

She waved.

Both Jeff and Holly started at the same time to introduce their friends to each other and this caused looks of amusement on both Tina and Kenny's faces.

They paused and Jeff tried again. "This is my friend, Kenny. We work together."

Before Holly could say anything, Tina stepped forward. "I'm Tina, Holly's lifelong friend."

Kenny spoke up. "We're heading out for a few beers, want to join us?"

"Sure," Tina said enthusiastically.

Holly looked at Jeff, mortified. She was pretty sure the expression on his face matched hers.

"We're just going to Hannigan's," Kenny continued. "Do you know where it is?"

"I do," Tina said. "We'll see you there." Tina bounded down the steps toward her car. Without looking back, she called out, "Come on, Holly, light a fire under it."

Holly gave a weak laugh and shrugged at both the guys. She turned and headed down the steps, wondering how she could extricate herself from this situation. She wanted to clock Tina on the head.

CHAPTER NINE

Jeff started his truck and pulled out of his driveway. He looked over at Kenny.

"What did you do that for?" Jeff asked.

Kenny looked at him oddly. "Do what?"

"Inviting Holly and her friend to join us," Jeff said pointedly. When he reached the stop sign at the end of the street, he threw on his indicator.

"Don't you know Holly? Isn't she your tenant?" Kenny asked, looking at Jeff as if he'd lost his mind.

"Yes, but I don't want her to think I'm stalking her," Jeff explained. In his rearview mirror, he saw Tina's car behind them.

"It's a drink, Jeff! We're not asking them to donate kidneys," Kenny said. "Is *not* having a drink with your tenant part of the lease agreement? It's a strict tenant-landlord relationship, then?"

"No, but you know what I mean," Jeff said.

"I don't, actually. I saw two pretty girls and I asked them to join us. Where's the problem?"

Jeff didn't answer right away, and Kenny reached over and turned the volume on the radio way up, cutting off any further protests for the rest of the drive. When they got close to Hannigan's, Jeff pulled into an open parking space and shut off the ignition. Tina's car passed them and pulled into a spot close to the entrance.

"We don't really know her friend," Jeff said, knowing it sounded lame even as he was saying it.

"You've got to be kidding me. What, do you think she might be a serial killer or something? Wanted by the police in three states? Do you need a reference to have a beer with someone?" Kenny asked. "This is how you get to know someone, Jeff. Come on, stop worrying and let's go inside. It's freezing out here."

Jeff locked up the truck and grumbled to himself as they headed toward the bar.

As soon as he opened the door, he was hit by a wall of noise, and a flash of panic coursed through him. Maybe he should just go home. He hated these types of situations. Loud music, crowds of people and now he was expected to make small talk with Holly and her friend, who he didn't even know. All he had wanted to do was watch the hockey game with his buddy.

"They're over there," Kenny said, slapping him on the arm and waving to acknowledge Tina's wave.

Jeff dragged his feet as he followed Kenny.

Kenny turned to him. "Will you come on? And perk up, for God's sake. You look like you're going to a funeral."

Jeff detected exasperation in his friend's voice. But he couldn't help it. He didn't do well in groups. Unknown variables made him anxious and right now that unknown variable was Tina. And by extension, Holly, as well. She might be a whole different beast, out socially and with a friend.

He pulled a chair out and sat next to Holly. The game was playing on the TV screen in the corner but he could forget about watching it. He couldn't be that rude. Kenny offered to go get drinks from the bar and took their orders. Jeff ordered a light beer for a change.

"Will I go with you to give you a hand carrying them back?" Tina offered.

Kenny smiled. "That'd be great."

The two of them went off together, chatting amiably. Jeff wondered how they did it. They made it look so easy. He turned to Holly. She seemed awfully quiet. Maybe she didn't want to be seen with him.

"How you doing, Hol?" he asked.

"Good." She smiled. "And you?"

"Fine," he answered.

"So, you work with Kenny?" she asked.

"Yeah, we started together at the same time. We were in the same training group."

Jeff looked toward the bar and saw Kenny and Tina, deep in conversation, holding two drinks apiece.

"They seem to be getting along," he remarked.

She nodded and the conversation fizzled out. Jeff looked around, wracking his brain, trying to think of something to say. Preferably something witty and clever.

"Look, Holly, I'm sorry about Kenny," he started.

She looked at him with a confused look on her face. "What do you mean?"

He looked around and lowered his voice. "Kenny can be kind of impulsive at times. I hope we didn't ruin your night out."

Holly's face relaxed and she shifted in her seat. "Don't worry about it, Jeff. To tell you the truth, I really didn't want to come but I let Tina talk me into it." She stopped and gave him a smile. "Truth be told, I'm glad you're here."

"Don't tell me you're a homebody like me?" he asked.

She nodded. "This really isn't my scene. When I was younger I went out a lot, but I don't know, I think you kind of outgrow the bar thing."

"I couldn't agree more," he said, although he'd never been into the bar scene, even when he was younger.

Holly's attention drifted to something in the distance. "What's wrong, Hol? You seem distracted tonight."

She sat up straighter, folded her arms in her lap and leaned forward against the table. She poured out the story about Grace Sanders and her family.

Jeff listened without comment and when she was finished, he said, "We were at that fire last night. It was awful. There's nothing left of the house."

Holly shook her head and Jeff thought she might start to cry. It upset him to see how upset she was.

"How is the family doing?" he asked.

"They're all okay, thank God. But they've lost everything."

"That's devastating."

"We had a meeting after work to see what we could do about a fundraiser for them."

"Right." An idea began to take shape in Jeff's head and he was just about to verbalize it, but Kenny and Tina appeared and set the round of drinks down in front of them on the table. He'd tell her about it later.

***

On his next rotation, Jeff went to the battalion chief's office and rapped on the door. The chief was heading toward fifty. He was a fair-haired man with a ruddy complexion and six kids at home. He indicated to Jeff that he should take the seat across from him.

"I wanted to run something by you, chief," Jeff said, sitting down and pulling the chair up to the desk.

"Always a good thing." The chief smiled.

"You know how we have this annual Christmas dinner every year—"

"The one you don't go to?"

Jeff looked sheepish. "Yeah, that's the one."

"Go on." The chief sat back and folded his hands across his belly.

"And how all the proceeds go to a charity we pick?"

The older man narrowed his eyes. "Yes?"

"There was a house fire over on Potomac the other day."

"I heard about it. Faulty electrical wiring. Total, complete loss."

"They had young kids. Kids young enough to still believe in Santa Claus."

Jeff's boss swivelled in his chair. "I get your idea, Kowalek. I'll put it to the general vote."

Jeff slumped in his seat. He could practically count on someone to vote it down. Every place, every job had people like that. They would be putting forward their own agendas.

The chief stood up and Jeff followed suit. "Look, Kowalek, I've got kids myself. Lots of them. And some of them still believe in Santa, too. So, I'll push for it in a way that it will get the okay and we can help those kids have a good Christmas despite everything."

Jeff grinned. "That's great, chief. I really appreciate it." He stood up, satisfied, and headed toward the door.

"Hold on a minute," his boss said. "I'm not finished."

Jeff pulled up short and stood in the doorway of the office, looking back.

"I'll push for it and make sure it happens, but only if you agree to attend the dinner."

Normally, Jeff would sigh and groan but at this point, he'd do just about anything to help this family out. And that was not limited to running down the street buck naked in broad daylight.

"I'll be there," he said.

"Good, I'll take care of it," the chief said.

***

"Aunt Holly, when are you going to put up your Christmas tree?" asked six-year-old Sarah.

Holly looked around her place. She supposed to a child it must look awful without a tree. She had a few sentimental decorations around her new home. There was the ceramic Santa and Mrs. Claus that had been her grandmother's and were more than sixty years old. There was the big snow globe with the snowman inside that had been the first holiday decoration she'd bought when she had moved out of her parents' house. Her younger niece, Emily, aged four, shook it constantly, watching the snow fall, never tiring of it. She had put on some Christmas music for the girls. They stood in Holly's kitchen in their footie pajamas, excited about the sleepover and the prospect of baking cookies. Holly turned on her brand-new oven to preheat it, then rolled out the dough for the cutouts. Her nieces pressed different forms into the dough, creating bells, stars, angels and Christmas trees. She lined them up on the baking sheets.

Suddenly, the smoke alarm started shrilly beeping, startling them. She looked toward the oven and her eyes widened in surprise when she saw smoke pouring out of it.

"Our alarm always goes off when Mommy cooks," Sarah said thoughtfully. Emily picked up a piece of scrap dough and put it into her mouth.

Holly ran toward the oven and opened the door, to be greeted by flames. There was a brand-new baking pan inside the oven wrapped in cardboard with a manual and safety instructions, all of which had caught fire. Holly thought about throwing water on it but wasn't sure. She flapped her kitchen towel at it, trying to wave out the flames. The smoke thickened. Behind her, Sarah dropped to the ground and began to roll away.

"What are you doing?" Holly cried.

"I'm stopping, dropping and rolling," the girl answered.

"Girls, go stand by the front door."

There was a knock at the front door.

Holly groaned in frustration. She was kind of busy, trying to put out a fire. "Who is it?" she barked.

"It's Jeff. Everything okay in there?"

"Girls, let him in."

Her nieces stood still. "Sarah, open the door," Holly instructed.

"We're not allowed to open the door to strangers," Emily said seriously.

"Jeff, it's open," she shouted.

The door opened, and Jeff entered, stopping short when he saw what Holly was dealing with.

"Get the extinguisher!" he said, running past the girls towards the utility room off the kitchen.

"I have one?" Holly asked, standing up from the oven.

Jeff returned with a fire extinguisher in hand. He pulled the clip and sprayed white foam over the interior of the oven, dousing the flames immediately. He crossed the room and opened the window, allowing the smoke to escape.

Holly stared at the mess of her new oven and felt her posture sag. She looked at the baking trays loaded with unbaked cut-outs. She looked at Jeff and asked wearily, "Can I use your oven again?"

***

Jeff and Holly, with the help of the girls, transferred the baking trays to Jeff's kitchen. Once the oven had preheated, Holly popped in the trays and set the timer on her phone. She watched as he questioned the girls about what they wanted Santa to bring them. Soon, Emily was jumping up and down with excitement, clapping her hands.

When the alarm beeped, Holly checked the cookies, and seeing they were done, removed them from the oven and placed them on Jeff's counter. She placed the two remaining baking trays in the oven and waited.

The girls sat on either side of Trixie, petting her and talking to her. The dog seemed unmoved but did lift her head at times to look at each girl. Holly briefly wondered if the animal was depressed.

Jeff approached her. "I have some news, Hol. I spoke to the fire chief about the Sanders family and he's agreed to let the proceeds from the annual Christmas dinner go to them."

Holly beamed at him. "Jeff, that is amazing! Thank you so much."

"It won't be enough to rebuild their house but it will be enough to buy some Christmas presents for the kids," he said.

She wanted to hug him but held back. "I can't thank you enough."

"Come on, I'll help you carry these back," he said, nodding toward the trays of baked cut-outs.

"Time to go, girls," Holly called, picking up two cookie sheets.

"Aw, we want to stay with Trixie," Sarah whined.

"You can visit her anytime," Jeff suggested.

They corralled the girls back to Holly's place. She and Jeff laid the cookies on the table. She looked at the mess that was her oven and sighed. One more thing to do.

As if reading her mind, Jeff went over and closed the oven door. "Leave it, Hol. If I have your permission, I'll come in when you're not here and clean it up."

Holly was mortified. "I couldn't ask you to do that." She watched as Jeff bent down and wiped up the floor in front of the stove with some paper towels. The muscles in his back rippled underneath his shirt with the effort. She forced herself to look the other way.

He smiled and shrugged. "You didn't ask me, I offered. Look, it's a process. I'm going to have to vacuum up the powder from the extinguisher first, then wipe it out and then use oven cleaner. I don't mind doing it."

She hesitated, unsure. "Well, all right, I guess."

There seemed to be nothing more to say but Jeff made no movement to leave. He'd just offered to clean out her oven, so she thought she should try to be a bit more hospitable.

"The girls and I are going to have some cocoa and decorate these cookies." She paused. "Would you like a cup?"

"Sure, if it's not too much trouble," he said.

She pulled down four mugs from the cupboard. While the kettle boiled, she laid out the baked cookies on the table, along with small bowls of icing. To each bowl, she added a different drop of food coloring: red, green, yellow and blue. She put bottles of colored sugar, silver balls and red and green sprinkles on the table.

The girls clapped their hands, excited.

"I'll do the first one so you can see how it's done," Holly said. She bent over the table and iced one of the cookies, aware of Jeff behind her, leaning against the counter with his arms folded, watching her. She put a light dusting of red sprinkles over her cookie. Her nieces watched, rapt. She looked at both of them. "Okay, your turn."

Sarah sat in one chair while her little sister knelt on another. Holly watched them, delighted over their eagerness.

She made up the cocoa and brought the mugs to the table. She handed one to Jeff.

She pulled out a chair and sat between the girls. "Jeff, sit down."

He joined them, sitting across from Holly.

"Here, Jeff, I made this one for you," Sarah said shyly, handing him a cookie. Holly was about to protest, as the cookie had about two inches of frosting and was covered in a pile of sprinkles.

"Thank you, it looks delicious," Jeff said good-naturedly, taking a bite. He chewed thoughtfully for a moment. "I think this may be the nicest Christmas cookie I've ever had. Do you bake a lot of these?"

Sarah giggled. "No, silly, I'm only a kid."

"Oh, I see," he answered.

"I want to make Jeff a cookie," Emily yelled. She laid a thick coat of icing on a star-shaped cutout and loaded the top with silver balls. Proudly, she handed it to Jeff.

"Wow, that's almost too beautiful to eat," he announced.

Emily beamed. Holly sipped her hot chocolate and watched Jeff interact easily with her nieces. He was a natural with kids. Her thoughts started to stray in an unwanted direction and she had to force them out of her mind. No matter what, she wasn't going there. She couldn't.

***

On Sunday night, Holly helped Emma carry the shopping bags inside. It was gift wrapping night. As she did, she glanced toward Jeff's side of the duplex, seeing lights on. Last night over cocoa and baked goods, they decided to pool their resources for the charity fundraiser for the Sanders family.

She laid the bags of toys on two of her kitchen chairs. The plan was to wrap all the Santa gifts for the girls and store them in Holly's spare bedroom. Her sister set her bags on the floor and draped her coat and purse over the back of a chair.

"Ugh, a night free from baths and stories and endless requests for a glass of water at bedtime. Is it me or do all kids get incredibly thirsty at bedtime?"

Holly laughed despite the resurfacing of an old, familiar pain. What she wouldn't give for a complaint like that. She pulled down a couple of wine glasses and uncorked the bottle of wine she'd picked up for the occasion.

"Red okay?" she asked.

"Fine, as long as it has alcohol content in it," Emma said. "Do you have tape and scissors?"

Holly nodded. "In the basket at the end of the counter."

Her sister pulled out multiple tubes of wrapping paper from one of her bags, all with varying patterns of Santa Claus, reindeer and snowman prints.

"So how is your landlord?" Emma said, pulling out the first toy to be wrapped.

"He's a real gem."

Emma stopped what she was doing and looked at Holly, raising an eyebrow. "Is there a romantic interest there?"

Holly immediately shook her head, wanting to disabuse her sister of any silly notions. She had enough on her plate as it was without adding a romantic entanglement with her landlord to the list.

"No, he's just a friend. Besides, he's not really my type," Holly pointed out.

"That's exactly what I'm getting at," Emma said. "Because your type hasn't really worked out in the past, has it?"

Holly ignored her and pulled the gifts out of the bags and laid them on the table. "Ooh, who's getting Barbie?" she asked, examining the doll.

Emma smiled. "They both are. It will make my life a lot easier. Let's put Sarah's presents on the counter and I'll wrap Emily's first."

"Who gets what?" Holly asked, looking at the bags of toys at her feet. She felt a little pang. She would love to be doing this for her own children but she didn't really see that in her future. She was barely getting by, she'd never be able to go all out for Christmas. At least not in this lifetime.

"Let's switch," Emma suggested. "I'll sort and you start wrapping."

Holly nodded and took her seat at the kitchen table. She took the first toy, studied it and smiled. Ah, to be a kid again. She measured out wrapping paper and began to cut it to size.

"Holly," Emma started.

Holly paused, scissors midair, and looked at her older sister.

"I think you should talk to Mom and Dad about everything and tell them how you feel," her sister suggested. "Well, with Dad more than anything. Clear the air, so to speak."

Holly immediately shook her head. "No way."

Emma sighed, frustrated. "Just hear me out. First, they're your parents, and I know Dad can be a pain in the ass sometimes but Mom cares. You know that. And even Dad cares in his own way."

"I suppose. It's just that I'll never hear the end of it," Holly said, taping up the present. "How I'm a failure... What was I thinking... It will go on and on and on. No thanks. I already feel bad enough as it is. I don't think I could feel any worse, but I know Dad would try."

"Instead of telling me this, tell Dad," her sister pointed out.

Holly's shoulders sagged. "I can't. But if I keep our contact to a minimum, I can handle it."

Her sister looked at her as if she'd lost her mind. "That's your plan? Stop seeing Mom and Dad so you don't have to deal?" Her sister stared at her, a stuffed animal in one hand and a set of plastic dishes in the other. She muttered, "You can't push them away."

Holly didn't answer her. She supposed it did sound a little outrageous but for the moment, she didn't have a better plan.

Emma asked quietly, "Would you like me to talk to him?"

"No, thanks," Holly said. She couldn't have her sister fighting her battles for her anymore, not like she had when they were kids.

Her sister waited, studying her. Holly relented and gave her a bright smile that felt false to her. "All right. I promise, I'll talk to them soon."

***

Holly was in a much better mood Monday morning than she had been in a while. She had had a lot of fun with her nieces baking holiday cookies despite the oven catching on fire and she'd spent some time helping her sister. Holly had mentioned the idea of working with the fire department for the fundraiser for the Sanders to Janet, who thought it was a great idea. It was decided that Holly would act as the liaison between the school and the fire station. She caught herself humming a Christmas carol as she unlocked the door to her classroom.

She had also decided the class Christmas craft project was going to be gingerbread houses this year. It was ambitious, but last night, in bed in the dark, she'd decided she wanted to do something fun for the kids, especially for Grace. She crafted an email asking for volunteers for the project and sent it out to the parents in her class.

The kids began to trickle in and Holly noticed Jimmy walking in with his head down. He wasn't his usual effervescent self. It was such a marked departure from his usual demeanor that Holly felt he bore watching. For the rest of the morning, he remained out of sorts. There had been no talking, no restless shifting in his seat and no staring out the window. She wondered if he was coming down with something.

As the bell rang for lunch, the kids excitedly jumped out of their seats, heading for the back of the class to retrieve their lunch sacks. Jimmy slid listlessly out of his own seat and pulled his lunch bag out of his backpack at the back of the room. He was one of the last kids left in the classroom, whereas he usually led the lunchtime stampede.

As he walked by her desk, she called out to him. "Jimmy?"

"Yes?" he asked, stopping in front of her desk.

"Are you all right?" she asked, eyeing him.

"Yeah, I guess," he said, his eyes downward.

"Are you sure?"

"Can I ask you a question?" he asked.

"You sure can."

He looked up at her, his face earnest. "Do you believe in Santa Claus?"

"Do I believe in Santa Claus?" she repeated. She knew there were some children in her class who still believed. Most did not. She wanted to be honest with him but he was only nine—she didn't want to be a Grinch. She sighed. She had to go deep within herself, past all the debris that was her life to find the right answer for him.

She came out from behind her desk.

"My mom told me last night there's no such thing as Santa Claus, that it's the parents who buy all the presents," he said. He put his head down and lowered his voice. "She said I was getting too old to believe in that kind of thing."

Holly sighed, her heart breaking, and bent down in front of him so that she was eye level with him.

"Actually, there once was a Santa Claus. He lived a long time ago and he used to give presents to all the children," she started. "And even though he's no longer with us, his memory lives on today in each and every one of us. The magic and generosity of Santa Claus is still alive today. Right here." She tapped her heart. "We keep Santa Claus alive within ourselves by our willingness to give to others and to be kind."

He nodded. A very small smile emerged on his face. "I never thought of it like that."

She smiled warmly at him. "Go on now, eat your lunch before break is over."

He headed out of the classroom, and when he reached the door, he looked back and said, "Thanks, Miss Fulbright."

CHAPTER TEN

On Monday evening, Holly was just taking out a pile of flattened cardboard from her few packing boxes as Jeff was rolling his wheelie bins to the curb. She waited for him, smiling. She hadn't seen him in a couple of days and it dawned on her that she had missed him.

"Just tuck it between the two bins, they'll take it. The fellas are good like that," Jeff said. "Of course, the bottle of whiskey I give each of them at Christmas probably helps."

Holly did as he instructed and straightened back up. She looked back to her side of the duplex. She hesitated but then found her nerve. "Do you want to come in for a cup of coffee or a beer?"

He shook his head. "I'd love to, but I can't. I'm actually going on a date tonight."

Holly felt disappointed but recovered quickly. "Well, good for you." And why shouldn't he go out on a date? He was a great guy. It amazed her that he was still alone.

He laughed. "I finally agreed to let Mrs. Peters set me up with her niece."

"Oh," Holly said, trying to process it.

"I'll let you know how it goes." He grinned.

She didn't think she'd want to know how it went. She felt a little twinge of jealousy and this surprised her. It had been a long time since she'd been interested in a man. She'd thought those feelings were long dead. She hoped, whoever the woman was, she would appreciate Jeff and all his wonderful qualities.

***

Jeff shaved and showered, whistling as he got ready. He slapped on a little cologne, feeling both excited and nervous. It'd been a long time since he'd been on a date. Longer since he'd been on a blind date. But it was time to make changes and most importantly, it was time to get out of his comfort zone. He didn't know what to expect that evening. But he'd decided he was just going to go with the flow. It would have been nice to take Holly up on her invitation for coffee—for a split second he'd even thought about canceling the blind date. But he'd never live with Mrs. Peters' wrath. Besides, Holly was probably just being polite, since he'd cleaned out her oven.

Trixie showed no interest as he got dressed in the bedroom.

"You know, you really need to get a life, too," Jeff said to her. "No more lying around. I think you need a boyfriend."

The dog groaned and turned her head away.

"Don't ignore me, Trixie, you know I'm right. I know you're listening," Jeff said, strapping his watch on his wrist. "I think it's time you and I went to the park."

The dog did not acknowledge Jeff in any way.

"Just think about it," Jeff said, and he turned out the light and left the room.

***

Holly closed the door behind her, the nagging sensation of Jeff going on a date settling like a big stone in her stomach. It was a perfectly reasonable thing for him to do. Some other woman being interested in him was a logical conclusion, she thought bitterly.

Her thoughts were interrupted by her ringing phone.

She glanced at the screen and swiped it to answer the call.

"Hi, Mom," she said.

"Hi, Holly. I haven't heard from you in a while so I thought I'd give you a call and see how you were getting on in your new place."

"Fine, Mom," she answered. She felt a sudden stab of guilt. Between teaching, working three shifts a week at the restaurant and trying to get settled in her new home, she hadn't had a lot of time or energy left to do the things that needed to be done. Namely, staying in touch with her parents. Well, her mother, at least.

"Your father wants to know when we can come over and see your new place," her mother said.

Holly panicked at the thought. She wracked her brain for an excuse but could not come up with one.

"Can we stop over tomorrow night?" Gloria asked.

Holly sighed in resignation. It was her night off. She had no reason to refuse them.

"To make things easier on you, we can bring some dinner with us," her mother suggested. Holly thought she detected sadness underneath her tone.

She closed her eyes and decided to bite the bullet. "I'd love to see you. Be here at six and I'll cook the dinner."

Her mother could not hide her surprise, and when Holly reassured her she didn't mind cooking, Gloria couldn't hide her delight.

When Holly hung up, she collapsed on the sofa, wondering what she had just gotten herself into.

***

Mrs. Peters had arranged for Jeff to meet her niece outside the restaurant. Jeff decided to give Trudy a chance and in return, he hoped she'd do the same. The restaurant was all done up in Christmas decorations and as he waited outside, he whistled along to the holiday tune being played over the loudspeakers.

He glanced at his watch, noting he was right on time. He'd once had a girlfriend, Chrissy, who couldn't be on time to save her life. It was a trait that had annoyed him to no end. He thought of all the hockey games, football games, movies and just about everything else where they'd arrived late and missed the beginning. He'd been relieved when the short-lived relationship had broken up. Surprised, but definitely relieved. It had meant he could go back to being punctual. Even if it did mean he'd ended up being alone.

"Jeff?"

His head snapped up and he came face to face with an attractive woman about his own height, with shoulder-length dark brown hair and dark brown eyes. She had a gap between her front teeth that Jeff thought was kind of sexy.

"Trudy?" he asked in return.

She nodded. His first impression was positive. And there was hope, as she hadn't bolted at the sight of him. Yet. He wanted to kick himself. Mrs. Peters had been trying to fix him up with her niece since he'd moved into the neighborhood five years ago. And he had always begged off. Well, no more being afraid, he thought. Tonight, he was going to make up for lost time.

They walked through to the foyer of the restaurant and Jeff asked the hostess for a table for two.

When they were seated, the server handed them each a menu. Without opening it up, Trudy laid hers down on the table and announced, "I know what I'm ordering."

"Really?" Jeff asked. "Already?"

She smiled. "I eat here a lot. I always get the same thing."

"Don't you ever want to shake it up and get something different?" he asked, playing devil's advocate, knowing full well that prior to his cardiac event, he would have cut off his arm before deviating from his own script.

She shook her head. "Nah. If I order what I already know I like, I won't be disappointed."

"True," he said, scanning the selection of steaks, his own default choice. He forced himself to look at rest of the menu, thinking that just this once, he wanted to try something different.

She ordered a chicken dish and Jeff opted for the tuna. They agreed to ordering a bottle of wine.

"So, tell me about yourself," Jeff said, trying to sound smooth but thinking it sounded corny. He tried not to wince.

Trudy smiled and Jeff thought hers was a face he could get used to.

"Well, I've just turned thirty and I work at Bluff Falls City bank," she said.

"Do you like your job?" he asked.

"Oh, I do. A lot," she said with enthusiasm.

"You sound passionate about it—that's great," he said. "What do you like about it?"

"Looking after people's money is an important job. Most people care more about their money than they do their health," she opined.

He had to agree. How often had he listened to Morty complaining about bank fees?

She leaned forward and whispered, "Plus you get the inside track on everybody's financial business."

He frowned, hoping she didn't mean what he thought she meant.

The waiter arrived and poured their wine for them. Jeff took a gulp.

"For instance, the owner of this place has maxed out his emergency overdraft," she whispered. She sat back and nodded knowingly.

"Well, it's a good thing we ordered appetizers, then. We should probably order dessert, too," he said, a little uncomfortable having this knowledge. "Should you be telling me this?"

She shrugged and waved her hand. "You look like the sort who doesn't go blabbing everyone's business."

Unlike yourself, he thought.

"Do you know the mayor and his wife?"

Jeff nodded. "I'm on the city payroll, so I've seen him once or twice."

"Well, his wife has opened up an account in her own name and has been siphoning money from their joint account. Building a little stash for herself. And he's got an election coming up."

Jeff began to squirm in his seat. He was thankful his own account was at a different financial institution.

The server set their appetizers down in front of them.

Jeff decided to change the subject.

"Have you ever been married?" he asked. He wanted to get as far away from the subject of the bank as possible.

"No, but close," she said. She sneered and Jeff found this ominous. "He dumped me three weeks before wedding."

"Oh, that's tough," Jeff said, digging into his caprese salad. It was quite good, actually. Holly had been right. Salad could taste good.

Trudy smirked. "Oh, don't feel sorry for me. He got his comeuppance."

Jeff was afraid to ask but couldn't help himself. "What do you mean?"

"I'm a big believer in karma and the laws of the universe," she said. She picked up a stuffed mushroom and offered it to him. "Do you want to try one? They're delicious."

Jeff shook his head. "No thanks."

"Anyway, sometimes the universe needs a little help in the 'what goes around, comes around' department," she said. "Let's just say that sometimes I like to drive the karma bus."

He looked at her oddly.

"I fiddled with his bank account."

Jeff looked at her in horror. "You didn't!"

"Oh, yes, I did." She smiled. "I did a 'bank error in your favor' type of thing."

"I don't get it," Jeff said.

She rolled her eyes as if already tired of the subject. "I took a deposit and transferred it into his account instead of the rightful one. And I waited for him to spend the five thousand, as I knew he would." Here she rolled her eyes. "He was always so predictable. Then I alerted the bank to the error, leaving him in a bit of a hole." She sat back, beaming, proud of herself.

Jeff tried not to appear horrified. He was pretty sure what she had done was some kind of federal crime. The movie *Fatal Attraction* came to mind and he was grateful that Trixie was too big to fit into a pot.

This woman was nuts, and not in a good way.

Although anxious to get out of there, Jeff ordered dessert, thinking about the beleaguered owner of the restaurant and his maxed-out emergency overdraft.

As the date wore on, Jeff began to think she wasn't so attractive, after all. The gleam in her eye took on a psychotic look and he wished she'd push back her hair so he could see if she had low-hung serial killer ears.

He walked her to her car, trying to figure out how to disengage himself from this situation and all the potential disaster that awaited him. He would love to have a girlfriend, but he didn't want to end up memorialized by a chalk outline.

"So, Trudy," he started.

She turned quickly to face him. "Look, Joe—"

"It's Jeff," he interrupted.

"Sorry." She gave him a small smile. "You're really nice. But this isn't going to work."

He was taken aback. The nutcase didn't want to see him again. If he were smart, he would feel relieved. But there was an odd sense of offense. What did it say about him if someone as unstable as her didn't want to go out with him again? "Oh. Okay."

She glanced around the parking lot, making sure no one else was in earshot.

"I really did this as a favor for my aunt," she explained.

He looked at her, uncertain.

"Aunt Peggy kept telling me how you'd seen my picture at her house and had been begging her to set you up with me," she said.

Jeff raised his eyebrows, slightly miffed. He had never even seen a photo of Trudy at her aunt's house. Mrs. Peters had been telling some porkies. He reminded himself never to string up Mrs. Peters' Christmas lights again. Maybe string up Mrs. Peters, but definitely not her lights.

"I'm sorry to let you down," she said.

"No, no, it's okay," he said, scraping slush back and forth with his boot. He realized he had dodged a serious bullet.

"Well, goodnight, then," she said. She pulled her keys out of her purse and clicked the remote to unlock her car.

"Wait a minute, Trudy," he said.

"Yes?"

"What made you change your mind and decide to go out with me?"

She shrugged and laughed. "I don't know. Christmas and all that. The season to be nice." And she got into her car.

He walked away feeling like someone's charity case.

***

Holly was planted on her sofa, watching television when she heard a knock on her front door. She stood up and lowered the volume on the tv. Glancing at the clock, she wondered who it could be. Before answering the door, she peeked out the front window and saw Jeff standing there. She'd thought he'd been out on a date.

She tied the sash around her fluffy pink robe and opened the door.

"Is your offer of coffee still on?" he asked.

"It went that well, huh?" She grinned. She held open the door for him and invited him in.

She started the coffeemaker, then placed two mugs down on the table and opened up a package of store-bought Christmas cookies. She sat down across from him, reached for a cookie and bit into it.

"So, tell me about your date."

He grimaced.

Holly smiled sympathetically. "That bad?" She pushed the carton of cookies toward him.

"Let's just say she's very passionate about driving a bus."

She frowned, not understanding, and he muttered, "Never mind." He proceeded to tell her about his evening with the vengeful niece of Mrs. Peters.

By the end of it, Holly laughed, horrified. "Wow, she is awful!"

They stared into their coffee cups and Holly had to admit she was glad Jeff hadn't got caught up in that nightmare of a date.

"Jeff, could you by any chance get me a ticket to that firefighters' dinner?"

"No problem," he said. "How many do you need? Two?"

"Just one," she answered, wondering why he'd think she needed two tickets.

"Oh, okay. Actually, I have an extra ticket and you're welcome to it."

"I'll pay you for it," she said firmly.

"No, that's not necessary, I get them for free from the firehouse," he said.

He was quiet for a moment before making a suggestion. "We could even ride over together if you want."

She hesitated before answering, "That sounds like a plan."

They were both quiet, Holly unsure of what she'd just agreed to and suddenly feeling shy.

Jeff broke the silence. "You don't have your tree up yet," he remarked, looking around. "You're running out of time."

Holly shook her head.

He laughed. "What? Don't you celebrate Christmas? Or is it some kind of protest?" he asked.

"More coffee?" she asked, standing up from the table.

"Only if you're having some more," he said. He fiddled with the handle on his mug.

She pulled the pot off of the coffeemaker and refilled their cups.

"So why no tree?" he pressed.

She sighed. He was like a dog with a bone.

Finally, she said, "Not this year. I can't afford it." She took a deep breath. There, she'd said it. An uncomfortable silence loomed. She studied his reaction but his face remained impassive. He appeared to be processing what she had just said.

"I'm sorry, I didn't mean to stick my big nose into your business," he said quietly.

She shrugged and looked away, feeling the tears threatening to make an appearance.

"Look, if you want to talk about it, I'll listen. And if you don't, that's okay, too."

She supposed she should start talking about it. She looked at his warm brown eyes and the concern on his face and she felt he would be someone she could trust. And right now, in her life, that circle was really small. She sat back down and dropped her hands in her lap, folding them. She stared at them for a long time. When she lifted her head, her eyes were dry and she cleared her throat. "I'm broke."

CHAPTER ELEVEN

Holly paused, waiting for Jeff's reaction, and when there was none, she soldiered on. "I was living with my boyfriend, Tim. We were engaged. We've—we'd—been together for years. We planned on getting married so I didn't think it was a problem when he suggested joint bank accounts and joint everything: deed to our house, credit cards, the works." She took a breath and lifted her coffee mug, taking a gulp. "What I didn't know was that Tim had a very serious gambling problem. He ran up our credit cards and took out a second mortgage on our home. Eventually, I found out, but by that time the damage had been done."

Jeff looked concerned. "Wow, that's incredible. And absolutely awful."

She couldn't stop talking. It was as if a tap had been turned on. "What I didn't know was that he had been fired from his job for embezzling." Her voice went shaky. "His firm decided not to prosecute if he left and paid back the money. We had to sell the house to pay off his firm. In the end, we had to file bankruptcy. We lost everything. We had to sell our house, our cars, our furniture and my engagement ring. I'm thirty-two years old and I'm back at square one. Except now I have really lousy credit."

"I'm so sorry," Jeff said earnestly. "I didn't know."

"Not too many people do. Anyway, I'm on a five-year court-ordered payment plan. Two years down. Three to go. That's why I work at the restaurant two to three days a week, for the extra money."

"Oh boy." Jeff looked thoughtfully at her. "What happened to Tim?"

She shrugged and let out a brittle laugh. "Who knows? He took off right after the bankruptcy judgement. Haven't seen or heard from him since. Can't find him."

"But he is helping you pay everything back," Jeff prompted, lifting his mug to his mouth for another sip.

She shook her head. "No, he left me holding the bag."

Jeff looked shocked. "But all of this is his doing," he observed. "None of it was your fault."

She smiled thoughtfully at him. "That's nice of you to say, but not entirely true. I'm complicit by omission. I handed everything over to him. I didn't keep an eye on credit card bills or anything. I'm to blame, too, in a way." She paused and then added, "I couldn't even lease a decent apartment because I have such a poor credit rating."

"So, let me get this straight. You're paying off the entire debt yourself with no help from him?"

She nodded. "Because we weren't married, we had to file bankruptcy separately even though our debts were joint. When he disappeared, I went straight back to our lawyer and things were grim. Once Tim stopped paying, the trustee would ask the courts to dismiss his bankruptcy and it would return to the creditors, who could then start hounding me for payment because it was a joint account. It just seemed easier to pay his portion myself."

"Have you thought about calling the police?" Jeff asked.

She smiled but she felt hollow inside. "I did, actually. But as it's not a criminal matter, there was nothing they could do."

"Wow, that is awful," he said. "Okay, but you're paying it back and you're doing what you're supposed to be doing."

"But my life is ruined," she pointed out.

He shook his head. "I respectfully disagree. Ending up dead, that's when your life is ruined. There's no coming back from that." He thought of the things he had seen as a firefighter. The really stupid things people did that cost them their lives. She could come back from this. It would take time. And there would have to be sacrifices. But she could do this. "This is something that can be overcome," he said with finality.

She shrugged. "It doesn't feel like it. I feel like I can't come out from under it."

"That's because you're exhausted from working two jobs."

"For the first year after it happened, I was inert. I couldn't do anything. I rented an apartment that was more trouble than it was worth," she said. She looked around her new place. "I can't tell you what a relief it was to find this place."

"Can your parents help you out?" he asked.

She shook her head decisively. "They offered. In fact, my parents wanted to pay off our debts."

"But you said no."

"I can't take money from them. They worked hard all their lives. They're not responsible for my mess," she explained. "My father was really angry when I wouldn't take any help."

"You still have your teaching job?" he asked.

She nodded. "Yes, thank God. No one at work knows what happened."

"I'll never breathe a word to anyone," Jeff said sincerely, leaning toward her.

She sipped her coffee and took another cookie from the plastic tray. "I know."

"Okay, so mistakes were made."

"Definitely. Bad decisions. Bad choices."

"However you want to label it," he said. "Can I ask you a question?"

She nodded. "Sure."

"How's your health?"

She laughed, caught off guard. "It's good. Excellent."

"There's your starting point. You're in good health, which enables you to roll out of bed each morning to get to work and make repayment."

"I thought I'd be farther along at this point in my life," she confided.

Jeff snorted. "You're not the only one."

"To top everything off, in a weak moment, I invited my parents over for dinner," she confessed.

He grimaced. "Right, the cooking thing."

"Oh, yeah, there's that, too," she said as if just remembering it.

He laughed. "That's not the problem? What is it, then? Haven't you ever sat down to dinner with your mom and dad?"

She gave a small, mirthless laugh. "Well yes, but my father can be awkward. Difficult."

"Oh, I see," Jeff said. He helped himself to a cookie. "I haven't had one of these cookies since I was a kid."

"Well don't worry, you'll see a lot more of them. They're going to be a holiday staple around here."

They sat in companionable silence sipping their warm drinks.

***

Holly held her breath as Grace Sanders hesitated in the doorway of the third-grade classroom. It was her first day back since the fire. Holly's heart tightened at the sight of Grace and her mom. The little girl had bags under eyes and suddenly looked shyer and much older than she normally appeared. Her mother stood behind her with her hands on Grace's shoulders. Life's most recent events were clearly etched on Mrs. Sanders' face. Holly rushed over to them but not before she noticed her classroom of third graders, all eyes on Grace, curious and intense.

Holly met them in the doorway, standing in front of them with her back to the classroom, shielding them from prying eyes.

"Mrs. Sanders, how are you doing?" Holly asked softly.

The poor woman could only nod. She seemed shell-shocked.

"Where are you staying?" Holly asked quietly.

"Grace and I are staying with my mother, and Bruce and the boys are at his brother's house," she explained.

"Oh," Holly breathed, feeling defeated for the woman and her family. It was awful enough to lose their home and all their belongings, but to be split up added insult to injury. She knelt down in front of Grace, taking the little girl's hands in hers. "Grace, how are you doing?"

The girl shrugged and said in a voice that Holly barely heard, "All my books are gone."

"Oh Grace, I am so sorry." Holly glanced at Mrs. Sanders, who gave her a quick nod. She stood back up and gave Grace's hand a little squeeze.

"The principal has been so wonderful to us," Mrs. Sanders said. "She gave us a bag of clothes to get by."

That was Janet. "Good. I suppose you'll need everything."

The woman nodded. "Yes, we're starting from scratch."

Oh boy. Holly felt for them. She knew what it was like to be knocked back to square one.

"I just hope she doesn't fall behind," fretted the girl's mother.

"Don't worry about that, Mrs. Sanders. I've put a list together of things we've covered in class and I've managed to get her some notebooks and supplies. Some of the girls have been really good about photocopying their notes for Grace."

The woman looked as if she was going to cry. "How thoughtful."

"I'll spend the next few lunches with Grace going over some things to get her caught up."

"Thank you so much," Mrs. Sanders said.

"All right," Holly said to Grace. "Shall we get started?" She stepped aside and allowed Grace to enter the classroom. The little girl hesitated, nervously playing with the end of her blonde ponytail as she scanned the faces of her classmates. She said goodbye to her mother and slowly made her way down the first aisle to the back of the classroom. After hanging up her coat, she went quietly to her desk by the windows and slid slowly into her seat.

Mrs. Sanders left and Holly was just about to close the classroom door and get on with the day's lessons when a high-heeled boot thrust its way between the door and the frame.

Mrs. Hopkins. Holly inwardly groaned. She didn't need this today. The woman's sunglasses were perched on top of her head, showcasing her impeccably made-up eyes. She wore a brown suede jacket with faux fur trim. Holly suspected the diamond studs in her ears were real.

"Oh, Miss Fulbright, I'm glad I caught you," Mrs. Hopkins said.

"The bell has already rung, Mrs. Hopkins. I'm just about to start class."

"This will only be a minute," she said, like she did every time. "It's about Brianna."

Well, who else would it be about? Holly wondered. She certainly wouldn't be here for Jimmy. Though Holly wished Jimmy's parents would take only half the interest in their child Mrs. Hopkins had in hers. At the last parent-teacher conference, the boy's parents hadn't bothered to show up and when she called and asked if they'd like to meet another time, his mother had responded, "Is he failing?" When Holly had said no, she'd replied there was no need to meet.

Mrs. Hopkins was talking about some teaching method she had read about online which she was proposing Holly might want to employ in her classroom. She thought it might benefit Brianna. Holly tuned her out and looked around at the kids' faces. Many were beginning to squirm and fidget, and the noise level of the room had increased. It was time to wrap this up. Robin was right—what Mrs. Hopkins needed was a project. Something worthwhile to do. Holly's eyes landed on Grace, who sat quietly at her desk, staring out the window.

"Mrs. Hopkins," she started, cutting the woman off mid-sentence. "Can I ask your help with something?"

Mrs. Hopkins' startled look at having been interrupted was quickly replaced by curiosity. "Of course," she said eagerly.

Holly lowered her voice so the classroom couldn't hear her. "Do you know Grace Sanders?"

The woman appeared momentarily caught off guard at the rapid shift in conversation. "The girl whose house caught on fire? Brianna mentioned something. So heartbreaking. And at Christmas time, too."

"She's the blonde-haired girl in the third seat by the window."

Mrs. Hopkins moved slightly away from Holly so she could get a better look at the girl. As she locked eyes on her, Holly said, "The school is running a fundraiser in conjunction with the fire department's annual charity dinner."

Mrs. Hopkins raised one eyebrow. "My husband and I are big supporters of that charity dinner. Do you need help?"

"We sure do," Holly said earnestly.

"I'll go down to the office right now and talk to Janet," Mrs. Hopkins said. Without another word about her own daughter, she turned on her four-inch heel and walked down the corridor toward the principal's office. Clearly a woman with a mission.

Holly returned to her favorite place in the whole world: the front of the class. "Can we welcome Grace back?" she asked her students.

A soft, shy chorus of 'Hi, Grace,' floated around the room with the exception of Jimmy, who yelled out, "Great to have you back, Grace!"

Holly worried about Grace. She had worried about her even before the fire. The girl was a lovely, quiet child. Maybe too quiet. She always had her head stuck in a book and didn't really mingle with the other girls in that cliquey way girls had in the schoolyard. It wasn't that the rest of the class bullied her; they were a good bunch of kids. But the girls had stopped including her in things and when Holly had questioned Grace about this, the young girl had replied, 'I'd rather read.' So, when the kids were chasing a ball around outside at recess or hanging out in groups by the fence, Grace could always be found sitting in the grass with her head buried in a book, or on the rainy, cold days, at the lunch table in the cafeteria.

Holly bit her lip. Her own problems seemed increasingly insignificant.

"All right, class. Let's get down to business. All eyes to the front of the classroom," she said, opening up the PowerPoint presentation she had prepared.

CHAPTER TWELVE

Dinner with her parents went off better than Holly had expected. She'd decided to keep it simple and just make some spaghetti. She added a nice salad, garlic bread and a bottle of wine. Her father seemed impressed with her new place and Holly was able to relax a bit.

As she cleared the plates, her mother stood up and offered to help.

"That's okay, Mom, just relax," Holly said.

"I don't mind honey," she said, taking the empty salad bowls off the table and setting them on counter. "Dinner was delicious."

"Thanks, Mom. I'm just going to give these plates a rinse and we'll have some pie and coffee."

"Pie sounds good. What kind?" her father piped up from his seat.

"Lemon meringue," she said proudly.

Her father nodded.

The doorbell rang.

"Alan can you get that?" Gloria asked.

Her father marched to the front door, opened it and then closed it. He strode back to the kitchen. "It's your landlord and his mother," Her father said, scowling.

"Jeff?" Holly wondered what he was doing here. And why he had brought his mother? But still, she'd be glad to see him. "You can invite them in, Dad."

"Is that a good idea? He's your landlord."

"Dad!"

"Alan, just open the door," Gloria huffed.

Holly watched as Ginger barreled through the door first carrying a medium-sized wicker basket wrapped in cellophane.

"Holly! Oh, you have company," she said.

"I told you her parents were over for dinner," Jeff muttered. Then he mouthed to Holly, "Sorry."

Ginger turned to Alan and Gloria and introduced herself. "I'm Jeff's mother, Ginger Kowalek."

"And we're Holly's parents," Alan said. Holly didn't know if he was being sarcastic or not because with her father you just didn't know.

"I'm Gloria Fulbright and this is my husband, Alan," Holly's mother said.

Ginger turned toward Holly. "I just wanted to thank you for helping Jeff when he was hospitalized. He told me you took care of Trixie and that you helped him shop for some healthy food." Holly watched her mother raise an eyebrow and Jeff's face reddened. Ginger handed her the basket. There were all kinds of gourmet coffee and cocoa with cookies and truffles in it.

"Thank you, Mrs. Kowalek, but this isn't necessary. I was just being a good neighbor," she said.

"We need more people like you in this world," Ginger said.

"What happened to you, Jeff?" Gloria asked.

"Ah, it was nothing, just—"

"He almost had a heart attack!" his mother finished his sentence.

"But I didn't," Jeff pointed out.

The coffeemaker beeped behind her and Holly asked, "Would you join us for dessert?"

Both Jeff and his mother answered simultaneously.

"We'd love to," his mother replied.

"We can't," Jeff said.

Ginger waved him off and said: "Don't pay any attention to him."

Ginger began to tell the Fulbrights about her upcoming trip to Italy.

"I'd love to go to Italy," Gloria said.

"I'm not leaving a perfectly good bed for a possible lousy one," Alan said. Gloria rolled her eyes.

The three of them landed on the sofa and Gloria began to ask Ginger about her trip.

Jeff turned to Holly. "I'm sorry for barging in like this. I told my mother you had company."

Holly smiled. "Jeff, don't worry about it. It's fine."

"Can I help?" he asked.

"Can you get mugs down for coffee? Does your mom drink coffee?"

Jeff nodded.

Holly sliced up pie and plated it, watching Jeff out of the corner of her eye. He brought down mugs and took spoons out of the drawer. She almost sighed looking at him. She was glad he was here. But she warned herself not to get to attached to him. She didn't think he was interested in her at all.

Jeff joined Holly at the kitchen counter, watching his mother and her parents seated in the living room. His mother sat in the only armchair Holly had and Mr. and Mrs. Fulbright were next to each other on the sofa.

He lowered his voice so that only Holly could hear. He sounded like a television announcer at a golf game. "And in one corner, coming in at a size sixteen, we've got Ginger Kowalek, who in her free time draws on her eyebrows in such a way that she looks like she's in a perpetual state of surprise. In fact, Ginger has been in a never-ending state of disbelief since the birth of her son over thirty years ago."

Holly elbowed him and giggled. "Shh. They'll hear you."

"Holly!" Alan Fulbright barked. "How's the pie and coffee coming? Don't make it your life's work."

Jeff looked at her and raised his eyebrows. "As you were. I got this."

Jeff took a plate of pie and a cup of coffee over to Alan Fulbright.

He returned and grabbed two more plates and handed one to Gloria and one to his mother.

Jeff took two chairs from the kitchen table and set them down in the living room. Holly carried in a tray with mugs of coffee on it as well as a bowl of sugar and a small jug of milk. She set it on the coffee table.

"So. Ginger—what is that short for?" Alan asked.

Jeff's mother's mouth opened slightly and she asked, "What is what short for?"

"Ginger," Alan said.

"Yes?" she asked, adding some sugar and milk to her cup of coffee.

Holly watched as her father hung his head in frustration and sighed.

Jeff rescued him. "Ginger is her real name. It's on her birth certificate."

"Oh, *that's* what you were asking. Why didn't you say so?" Jeff's mother said.

Alan opened his mouth and then thought better of it. He set his plate and mug down on the coffee table. He leaned back in his chair and folded his arms across his chest again. "We always had little Pekingese dogs named 'Sugar,' 'Clove,' and I think there may even have been a 'Ginger.'"

"Interesting," Jeff said, pressing his lips together. "But I can assure you that my mother is not a dog."

"I meant no offense," Alan said a little too loudly.

"And none was taken," Ginger added, looking markedly at Jeff. "Easy, Jeff."

Holly spoke up. "We're having a fundraiser on the twenty-first at the firehall for the family of one of my students, whose house burned down."

"Oh, how dreadful," Gloria Fulbright said, finishing her pie. "When did you say it was?"

"It's this Sunday, Mom," Holly said. "There's going to be a spaghetti dinner along with a Christmas gift auction."

"It's in conjunction with the annual charity dinner that the firefighters hold each Christmas," Jeff added. "Doors open at two for the dinner and the auction starts promptly at five."

"Well, you can count us in," Gloria said.

"But I might be busy that day," Alan protested.

"I doubt it," his wife replied.

"That's great. I'll make sure you get tickets," Jeff said. "What about you, Ma?"

"Morty and I have our disco party that night," Ginger said.

"What is that?" Gloria asked.

"Oh, it's a lot of fun. We all dress up in seventies' styles and they play disco music. We go every year."

"Ha. That's where disco music should have stayed—in the seventies," Alan said.

"I think it sounds like a lot of fun," Gloria said, ignoring her husband.

"Doors open at two for the dinner," Jeff said.

"Okay, Jeff, the disco party doesn't start until six, so we'll stop on our way," Ginger said.

"That's great, Mrs. Kowalek, we need all the support we can get," Holly said.

Holly stood up and refilled everyone's cup with coffee. Jeff cleared some plates.

"You're pretty familiar around here, Jeff," Alan Fulbright remarked, sipping his coffee.

Holly noticed a grim set to her mother's lips. Even Ginger paused and looked between the two of them.

"That's because we've become friends," Holly explained, smiling tentatively at Jeff, hoping he'd agree with her assessment. He smiled in return.

"Jeff, can I give you a little advice?" Alan asked, and before Jeff could answer, he plowed on. "Never mix business with pleasure."

"Thanks for the tip," Jeff said evenly.

"Were you this helpful with your previous tenant?" Alan pressed. Holly didn't miss the suspicious tone in his voice. Her heart sank. Her father was about to go on a tear. She recognized the signs.

It was Ginger who spoke up. "Oh, yes. Jeff's previous tenant didn't drive, so Jeff was always helping out with rides and errands and so on."

"So your tenant became more than a tenant?" Alan asked. Ginger looked at him, confused. Gloria elbowed him so hard that he emitted an 'oomph.'

Horrified, Holly stared at Jeff. But he seemed to take it in his stride. Not backing down, he said, "Well, yes, Lloyd did become more than a tenant. He became a very good friend, right up until he died at age eighty-three."

Alan only paused for a moment. "It could get very awkward if you were to become involved with my daughter. I mean, what would happen if you were to break up? You'd still be stuck with her as a tenant."

Holly felt her composure begin to waver.

Jeff looked at her with an expression that said 'I got this.' "I can assure you Holly and I are not in a relationship. She's a neighbor and a friend." He added, only half joking, "Is that allowed?"

"Not a good way to conduct business. You're friends and pretty soon the tenant is taking advantage. Late with the rent. Then they're asking for impossible upgrades. Keep your clients at arm's length is what I say."

Abruptly, Gloria Fulbright stood up from the table and announced, "That's it, we're going."

Alan looked up at her sharply. "Going? But I was going to have another slice of pie!"

She removed his coffee cup from his hand and said, "You're done. You can't play nice. Get your coat."

Holly stood there, shell-shocked.

Gloria shrugged on her winter coat. "Ginger, it was lovely to meet you. I hope to see you again. Jeff, take care of yourself."

Ginger was trying to process all that was going on. She looked back and forth between everyone. "Is it okay if I finish my pie?"

Holly smiled at her. "Take your time, Mrs. Kowalek."

Gloria hugged her daughter goodbye. "Thank you, Holly, for inviting us to dinner. It was lovely." The she took her by the arm and gently walked her to the front door. "Don't be such a stranger. Come over and see me sometime. I promise to lock your father in the basement."

Holly threw her arms around her mother and hugged her. "Thanks, Mom."

Alan Fulbright cleared his throat. Gloria disengaged from the embrace and without looking at her husband, headed out the door into the cold winter's night.

"Thanks, Holly, for dinner," he said gruffly, and he disappeared through the front door.

***

The following evening, Jeff stood at his door, leash in hand, trying to coax Trixie outside.

"Come on, it'll be a short walk, just up and down the street and then right back home," he said. But the dog wouldn't budge. "I promise we'll come right home." He wondered whether he should offer her a treat and he was just about to go back inside and get a dog cookie when Holly appeared on her side of the porch.

She wore a white ski jacket with her dark hair spilled out from under her green. She looked so pretty he was momentarily speechless. He thought Fernando was a lucky man.

"Hi, Jeff," she waved.

"Hi, Hol," he said. "I'm trying to take Trixie for a walk."

Holly walked over and peeked inside Jeff's house at his recumbent dog. "Not interested, huh?"

"Nope."

"Have you tried bribing her a with a treat?" she asked.

"I was just about to," he said. He ran back inside and pulled the box of dog biscuits out from the cupboard. He gave it a hard shake and the dog lifted her head up in his direction. She stepped slowly down from the couch.

"Now I've got your attention," he said. He rejoined Holly at the front door and waved the treat in front of the dog. Interested, Trixie followed him to the door.

"Wow, she's a slow walker," Holly observed.

Jeff looked at her. "Oh, Trixie doesn't do anything fast."

The dog eventually made it to the door, where Jeff clipped the leash onto her collar. Holly petted the dog. The dog ate the cookie and then looked outside as if she'd only just seen the front yard for the first time.

"Do you mind if I join you?" Holly asked. "I was about to go for a quick walk myself to clear my head."

"Sure," Jeff said, delighted.

Jeff led Trixie down the porch steps and headed toward the street. The sidewalks were covered in about two feet of snow but the road had been plowed and the asphalt was only wet.

They walked in silence for a few houses, both watching the dog as she ambled in front of them.

It was Jeff who spoke first.

"Kenny wanted to know if we could all go out together again. You, Tina and me."

She hesitated and he spoke hurriedly, horrified that he might have overstepped an imaginary boundary. "It was just an idea. Forget I mentioned it."

She laughed. "Relax. It's just not in my budget, Jeff. I wouldn't mind getting together again but I'd prefer to stay home."

Jeff nodded quickly. "We could get together at my house. Who says you have to go out to drink?"

Holly brightened at that suggestion. "That's a much better idea."

"Maybe we can get a game of naked Twister going," Jeff joked. When Holly blanched in response, he quickly backpedaled. "I was just kidding. It was my attempt at humor. A poor one."

She giggled and he was relieved.

"We'll get together and everyone will be fully clothed," he added quickly.

Their breath came out in steamy wisps as they walked on.

"Can I stick my nose in your business?" Jeff asked.

"Go ahead."

"Is your father always like that?" he asked, referring to the previous night. He'd thought her mother was nice but her father came across as abrasive.

"Unfortunately, yes. I don't know what makes him so difficult."

The asphalt, although wet, wasn't icy. Streetlights illuminated their way as they headed around the block.

They walked for a bit in silence, each thinking their own thoughts.

"My father is not a very affectionate man. Actually, he can be very critical."

"I may have noticed something along those lines," Jeff remarked.

"Do you know how I know that I'm doing what I'm supposed to be doing? How I know my father's proud of me?" she asked.

Jeff shook his head.

Holly let out a big sigh. "When he's not critical, when we can get through a conversation or a meal or whatever, without him nit-picking at me or how I'm living my life, then I know I'm off his radar."

Jeff didn't say anything. He didn't know what to say.

She continued. "All the years I was with Tim, I felt like a success. I had a good job. My fiancé had a good job. We had a nice home. And we saw my parents regularly. It was during those years my father was most accessible. He never praised me—he never would, he's just not that kind of man—but for the first time in my life, there was hardly any criticism," she explained. "I don't expect you to understand this, but I'm trying to tell you where I'm coming from."

Jeff frowned. "Geez, and I thought it was bad that my father walked out on me when I was three."

Holly stopped. "That is bad, Jeff. I'm sorry."

"No, no, there's nothing for you to be sorry about. I didn't mean to interrupt. That's a story for another time. Please, go on." They resumed walking.

"Well, when I first found out about Tim's deceit, I admit, I tried to cover it up. I stuck my head in the sand. I was overwhelmed. I had loved this man and he had betrayed me. I pretended, especially to my parents and probably on some level to myself, that everything was still all right. But when Tim disappeared, it was a charade I could no longer keep up. So, I went over to my parents' one night to explain to them what had happened. But when I told them, my father was so angry..." Holly paused.

It seemed to Jeff that the hurt was still that fresh. They walked on. Jeff remained silent, giving her space and time.

"He was so angry, said I was stupid to let something like that happen to me. He said other things, as well. It doesn't matter what, because I know he didn't mean half of it, but let's just say that sometimes words are weapons of mass destruction. After that, it was just easier to keep my distance," she said. "Nothing is black and white, you know? I love my dad, but love is rarely straightforward and can actually, in my opinion, be very difficult."

They walked on in silence the rest of the way.

***

They rounded the corner and Holly could see the duplex in sight. The walk had done her good; she had vented but now she felt exhausted. When they arrived at their duplex, Jeff spoke first.

"Well, don't give up on love yet."

She shook her head. "If you're referring to romantic love, I might just be done with that. After Tim, I don't know if I'll ever trust a man again."

They stopped in front of their duplex. The snowscape glittered under the shine from the streetlights. The snow crunched under their feet as they walked up the driveway. The dog, with the house in her sights, pulled on the leash.

"You can't give up, Hol," Jeff said again.

"Well I haven't given up," Holly responded, slightly irritated that he should be lecturing her. He stopped and looked at her as if challenging her.

She looked back at him. "What?"

"Just because you're breathing doesn't mean you haven't given up," he pointed out.

She scowled. "What does that mean?"

"What it means is that yeah, you've had a rough two years. There's no denying that. Mistakes were made. But you've got to pull yourself up by your bootstraps and get on with your life," he said.

She wanted to laugh but a frisson of anger traveled through her. "Bootstraps? Who even says that anymore?"

He shrugged and said quietly, "Well, apparently I do."

"You're hardly in a position to advise me or anyone else on being in a rut," she said sharply.

He flinched as if he had been hit. She wanted to kick herself for putting that look on his face. She was many things—the last two years had proved that—but she wasn't mean.

He looked away, down the empty street. Houses were lit up in various configurations of Christmas lights. He turned back to her. "I'm exactly the person to be giving this kind of advice, because I don't want you to end up like me: alone and never leaving the house, with no life."

She didn't know what to say. She could protest but that would look weak and sound insincere. But he didn't give her a chance to respond.

"Good night, Holly," he said abruptly. He marched up his porch steps with Trixie at his side and let himself into his side of the duplex without looking back at her.

CHAPTER THIRTEEN

Jeff had a lunch date with Rosemary on Thursday, all set up by Kenny's mother. Again, as he got ready, he was hopeful. He had purchased some new clothes at the mall in an effort to look nice. The only thing that concerned him was that when he'd asked Kenny if he'd date her, Kenny had hesitated before finally saying, 'Sure.' It had not been very confidence inspiring.

It had been decided that a meet up for coffee was the way to go. Jeff didn't think he could go through the whole course of appetizers, entrees, and dessert again. This way it would be one cup of coffee if it wasn't going to work out and two cups if things looked promising.

Kenny's mom had told him Rosemary would be wearing a blue scarf. Jeff was glad to have a visual reference to work with. He parked his truck outside The Brew Company and climbed gingerly over a snowbank to the front entrance. He stomped the snow off his boots before going inside. Out of habit, he brushed his hair down with his hand, even though there wasn't as much to brush down as there used to be. He was immediately hit by the warmth and the smell of freshly ground coffee beans. He glanced quickly around and didn't see anyone with a blue scarf. His heart momentarily sank but he glanced at his watch and realized he was ten minutes early. The place was crowded so he claimed one of the last remaining tables, by the window. He sat down and stared at the snow-covered scene outside. Everything was covered in white. The sidewalks, the shop signs, the cars and the giant green wreaths that hung from the black lampposts. Even the midday sky was a bright white.

He saw her first. She wore a white coat with a blue scarf and a matching beret. Her blonde hair was tucked up under her hat. She had a pleasant face. He stood up when she entered the coffee shop. When she looked in his direction, he gave a small smile and wave.

She walked toward him, smiling. "Jeff?"

"Rosemary?"

She nodded and laughed. "Well, I'm glad we got that out of the way."

He gestured toward the counter with its sandwich and dessert case that ran the length of the restaurant. Above, on the wall, were large blackboards listing all the different types of coffees and teas. "What would you like?"

She appeared to be studying the blackboard seriously. "Um, I'll have a no-foam latte with whip and a shot of espresso, and one packet of sweetener."

"Huh?" he asked. "Maybe you better write that down."

She laughed. "Just kidding. Black is fine."

He grinned. "You got me. I was just beginning to wonder if you were going to be as complicated as your coffee."

She gave him a warm smile. "No."

"Two black cups of coffee. We'll probably ruin their day," Jeff said. "How about a sandwich or a dessert?"

"Are you having any?" she asked. She had nice blue eyes, slightly too close together but overall good, he thought.

He shook his head. "Nah, I can't. Have to cut back. Doctor's orders."

"Then coffee's fine for me, too," she said.

"Seriously, Rosemary, get dessert if you want," he said.

She shook her head. "No, the coffee will be fine."

He caught himself whistling along with the Christmas tune being piped in overhead as he strode up to the counter. He had a good feeling about this one. As he paid for the coffee, an image of Holly flashed across his mind and he was disturbed by that. He didn't want her ruining his date.

Forcing her out of his mind, he made his way back to the table and set down their coffees.

She glanced at her watch. Jeff but couldn't help but wonder if she was planning her getaway.

She chuckled and said, "You should see the look on your face. I only looked at my watch because I'm on my lunch hour."

"Oh, all right. How much time do you have?"

"Forty-five minutes."

"That should give us enough time to get to know the basics."

She smiled. "Does that include whether we want to see each other again?"

He stirred his coffee, watching it swirl, and grinned. "I guess it does."

***

Later when he climbed into his truck to go home, his phone beeped.

Had a lovely time. Looking forward to meeting up with you again.

He responded, *Me too.*

***

Holly drove over to her parents' house after school finished Thursday afternoon. Her sister Emma was right. She couldn't keep avoiding her parents forever. She didn't bother calling; she'd thought she'd surprise them. Her class was making their gingerbread houses on Friday before school let out for Christmas vacation and she didn't have enough parents to help with the project. She worried about this on the ride to her parents' house.

The large two-story house where she grew up came into view and she felt her insides turn to lead. All her life, she had watched how hard her parents had worked, and now they were enjoying the fruits of their labors. They were comfortable and they wanted for nothing. She had wanted that kind of life for herself. She had thought she was playing by the book, working hard like her parents had taught her, but it had all gone so horribly wrong. Lesson learned.

She pulled her car into the drive, following it around to the back of the house. Everyone who knew the Fulbright family knew to come in through the kitchen. The front door was for strangers. She sat for a moment, gathering her courage, and eventually, forced herself out of the car.

She knocked on the back door and walked in. Both her parents were there in the kitchen. Her mother was sitting at the table, peeling vegetables with a stock pot at her side, and her father was pouring himself a cup of coffee.

"Hi, Mom, hi Dad," Holly said nervously.

"I just said to your mother, I wondered how long you were going to sit out there in your car," her father said by way of a greeting.

She smiled weakly, trying to not to lose her nerve.

"Holly, what a pleasant surprise," her mother said, putting down her peeler and wiping her hands on a towel. "Will you have some coffee? I've got a lovely apricot Danish here as well."

Holly sat down at the table. Her stomach growled in response. "That would be great."

Her father lowered himself into the chair across from her. "To what do we owe the pleasure of your company? This is twice in the same week that we're seeing you."

"Nothing. I just thought I'd stop over and see how you were doing."

Her mother spoke up. "And we're glad you did." She paused and looked at her husband. "Aren't we, Alan?"

"Of course we are. We're always glad when our girls stop by and see us."

Her mother brought over the coffee pot and two mugs, pouring one for daughter and one for herself.

"So, you're still at the restaurant?" Alan asked.

"I am. I'll be there for at least another three years," she answered. She got up and brought over plates and forks. Her mother set the Danish on the table and began to slice it up and pass it around.

"If you'd let me help you out, you wouldn't have to kill yourself working two jobs," her father started.

Holly closed her eyes. "Again, I appreciate your offer, but no thanks."

"Why not?" he asked. "Look, it can be a loan if it makes you feel better."

"Dad, please," Holly said.

"Alan, leave it," her mother warned him.

"I'm just trying to help," he protested.

"I appreciate it, but you can help me in other ways," she said.

"How?"

She smiled at him. For a moment she felt sorry for him that he had to ask. She was about to say something flippant, like 'Use your imagination,' but saw it as an opening to bridge the gap that existed between herself and her father. Here was her opportunity to say what she felt. And to clear the air as her sister was always advising her to do.

"Do you really want to know?"

"Yes," he said firmly. "I'm your father. I want to help my daughter."

She decided to give him the benefit of the doubt. "Two things. Sometimes, I would like advice but am afraid to ask."

Alan snorted. "That's ridiculous. Why would you be afraid?"

"Be honest with him, Holly," her mother directed.

"Sometimes, you can be very critical," Holly said.

Her father crossed his arms over his chest and blustered, "I'm just trying to help you get ahead by pointing out what you're doing wrong."

Holly raised her eyebrows. "But that approach doesn't help me. I'm all for constructive criticism, but I need positive support."

Alan Fulbright looked lost. He looked to his wife for help.

"She means listening without sarcastic comments and offering helpful advice," Gloria explained. "When asked."

Alan sipped his coffee. "Listening without sarcastic comments and offering helpful advice when asked," he repeated.

"Yes," Holly said.

"That's it?" he asked.

"For now," she answered, smiling.

"I'll take it under advisement," he announced. "But you know you can come to me any time for financial help."

"I know that, Dad. And thanks."

Holly looked around her parents' kitchen. It was spacious and welcoming, always full of delicious smells and lovely food to eat. Everything from the Delft tiles on the shelf to the expensive kitchen appliances indicated a life of comfort and abundance, and Holly all at once felt sad that she would never have that in her life.

"We're always here if you ever need us," Gloria said. "I hope you know that."

"I do, Mom," Holly started. "Actually, I do need some help with something."

Her mother waited, expectant.

"I'm doing a class project for Christmas. We're doing gingerbread houses."

"Sounds wonderful!" Her mother clapped her hands.

"We're doing it tomorrow, before they leave for Christmas break. But the problem is I don't have enough parents to help out. Most of them work," she explained. Although Mrs. Hopkins was going to be there. She had even emailed Holly with her own design ideas. "We need to do the project in two phases. In the morning, we're going to use icing to glue together graham crackers to make the walls and the roofs. And then in the afternoon, the kids are going to decorate their houses with candy.

Holly bit into her Danish, her mouth watering at the taste of the buttery pastry and the sweet apricot filling.

"Not a problem. What time do you need me there?" her mother asked.

"Thanks, Mom. Tomorrow morning at ten," she answered, washing down her Danish with coffee. "I know it's short notice but I had two parents email me today to say they couldn't make it after all."

Her mother waved her hand, "Don't worry about it. We're glad to help you out. And your father will come along, as well."

"Me?" Alan protested. "I don't know anything about making gingerbread houses."

"Use your imagination." Gloria laughed, picking up her coffee cup.

***

It was the last day of school before the Christmas holidays. There was a buzz in the air and it was contagious. Holly couldn't be in anything but a good mood. She had one more shift at the restaurant before Christmas and then she was off for the holidays.

Holly had been able to secure the art room for the making of the gingerbread houses. The first session involved using icing as adhesive to build the houses out of graham crackers. The parents who volunteered helped the children with this task. It was nice to see some fathers there, as well. Her own parents had showed up early, eager to help.

Her phone beeped when she was knee deep in icing and graham crackers and helping a couple of her students affix the icing to the sides of their houses. She glanced at it. It was from Jeff. She swallowed hard; she hadn't seen or heard from him since she'd insulted him the other night. She read the text quickly.

Dinner at my house tonight at seven with Kenny and Tina. Can you let Tina know?

She replied with a quick *Okay*.

"Oh," Jimmy groaned loudly. "The sides of my house keep falling in."

Holly was about to go to him but her father beat her to it.

"What's your name, son?" Alan asked.

The boy looked up at him. "Jimmy."

"Now, that's a great name for a kid," Alan said. "Why don't you put on the icing and I'll hold up the sides until they set."

Jimmy nodded and picked up the tube of icing.

After an hour, all the gingerbread houses were lined up on the windowsill by the radiator to allow the icing to dry.

Holly led the children back to their classroom where they had their Christmas party. The parents assisted with that, as well. They did their Secret Santa exchange and Holly watched, grateful, as the children of her third-grade class piled wrapped packages and gift bags on her desk. She was touched by their generosity.

Afterward, they headed back to the art room to put the finishing touches on their gingerbread houses. There were bowls of gumdrops, pretzels, licorice, and fruit flavoured candies. There were also bags of icing.

The volume of chatter was high and when they were finished, the children carefully carried out their gingerbread houses.

When they left, Holly and her parents stayed to clean up. Her dad went around the room with a big black trash bag and her mother wiped down the tables.

"I really enjoyed myself today," her mother said.

"Me, too," her father agreed. "They're all so excited. And they did a great job."

"They sure did."

"Hey, we should have the girls over to make gingerbread houses," her father suggested.

"They'd love it," her mother agreed.

***

Kenny arrived at Jeff's with two bottles of wine and a six pack of beer on Friday evening. When Jeff had mentioned to him about having dinner with Holly and Tina at his house instead of going out to a restaurant, Kenny had said it was no problem. Jeff sent Holly a quick text about the date and time and had asked her to let Tina know. She had responded with only an '*Okay.*' He hoped she wasn't feeling bad about what she'd said to him. He was over it but he didn't want her worrying about it, she had enough on her plate.

"What's for dinner?" Kenny asked.

"Grilled chicken and vegetables with roasted potatoes and a fruit salad," Jeff answered. He had spent a lot of time planning this meal. He'd added potatoes for the rest of the group. The fruit salad he was serving with a yogurt dip. He surprised himself with the fact that he was enjoying the cooking. He didn't even miss the fast food. Well, not too much.

"I'm starved," Kenny said. He set the wine on the counter and put the beer in Jeff's fridge.

Jeff was a little nervous about seeing Holly since she'd told him what she really thought of him the other evening. He probably still wouldn't be seeing her if Kenny hadn't pressed the issue of getting together. But he was determined to go forward with the dinner even if it meant some awkward moments between Holly and himself. He figured if his tenant had copped on after a month as to what kind of rut he was in, then he must truly be stuck.

"My mother wants to know how it went with Rosemary," Kenny asked, twisting off caps to two beer bottles. He handed one to Jeff.

"It was only a cup of coffee, but it went fine. She's a nice girl. We're planning on getting together again," Jeff told him.

Kenny laughed. "Finally! We may have found a girl for Jeff."

Kenny's teasing needled at Jeff. "It was only one date; it's hardly a commitment."

"Are you seeing her again?" Kenny asked.

"Yes," Jeff answered

"Then you're on your way."

The doorbell rang and Jeff was relieved. He wanted to get off the subject of Rosemary and any possible future with her.

"That'll be them," Jeff said. He answered the door and something in Jeff's heart seized as he caught sight of Holly. She wore a white ski jacket, pink hat and matching scarf, and her dark hair framed her pink-tinged cheeks. She had to be the prettiest girl he'd ever seen.

"Right on time, dinner's almost ready," Jeff said.

"Something smells good," Tina said, removing her coat.

Holly didn't say anything but she gave him a little smile.

Okay, so awkward it is, he thought. He took their coats and hung them up in the closet. Kenny poured Holly and Tina some wine. Jeff retreated to the kitchen and was grateful for the distraction of getting the meal on the table. Fifteen minutes later, he had everything plated up.

"Dinner is served," he announced.

Kenny sat across from Jeff, with Holly and Tina on the opposite side.

"It looks yummy," Tina gushed.

"I'm starving," Kenny asked her.

"Thanks," Jeff said. He felt surly. Holly hadn't so much as given him a glance. She spoke to Kenny and Tina but barely looked at him. He felt like a third shoe, not needed and definitely unwanted.

Tina spoke up. "So what is it like being a firefighter?"

"It's as you'd expect," Jeff answered. He ate some chicken, pleased with the results.

Kenny looked at him. "What kind of answer is that?" He turned to Tina. "I like it. It's a chance to help people. It can be dangerous at times, but someone needs to do it."

Jeff thought his friend would make a good PR person for the fire department.

"Did you ever see *The Towering Inferno*?" he asked Tina.

Tina speared some asparagus and shook her head. "I must have missed that one," she muttered.

"It was before you were born." Kenny smiled, winking at her. Tina blushed in response.

"Great movie, as far as disasters go," Jeff said, trying to get them back on point.

"Right up there with *The Poseidon Adventure*," Holly added.

"Exactly," Jeff agreed. Kenny and Tina exchanged a look.

"Anyway, in the movie, Steve McQueen is the beleaguered fire chief trying to fight this out-of-control fire in a skyscraper. Paul Newman is the architect of the building. Great movie."

"I must have missed that one," Kenny said, helping himself to more chicken. "This chicken is great, by the way."

"It's a good movie," Jeff said weakly.

"Lucky for us then that there aren't any skyscrapers in Bluff Falls," Kenny pointed out.

Silence descended. Jeff felt sweat break out on his hairline. He had cooked the dinner, he didn't think he should be expected to carry the conversation. Jeff wondered why on earth had he ever brought up a disaster movie? Him, small talk and social situations just weren't a good mix. It took nothing short of an act of God to prevent him from looking at his watch. He focused on his vegetables.

"Jeff, I think it's a great movie as well," Holly said softly.

He looked up at her and their eyes met and he felt a little bit of hope.

Kenny and Tina had started to talk about Christmas and Kenny was asking her what her plans were for the holidays.

After dinner, Tina stood up from the table and said she needed to use the ladies' room. Jeff directed her to the one off of the utility room.

He began the clean-up and he was encouraged when Holly stood up and began clearing plates.

At first, neither said anything. They worked in tandem: Holly clearing the table and Jeff loading the dishwasher. He noticed when Tina returned from the bathroom she and Kenny soon were in deep conversation.

Jeff nodded toward them. "They're getting on like a house on fire."

Holly looked toward them. "Yes, they are."

Holly scraped the plates off into the garbage can. She cleared her throat. "I want to apologize for what I said the other night."

He shrugged, trying to appear casual. But he was relieved. He'd thought she was angry at him. "It's all right, Hol."

She looked at him and shook her head. "No, Jeff, it's not all right. It's not how friends treat each other."

He smiled. "So, we're still friends?"

She looked shocked. "Of course we're still friends—why wouldn't we be?"

He shrugged again. "Anyway, you only spoke the truth."

"No, I didn't," she protested. "Since you went into the hospital, you've been making an effort to improve your life. And what, after only a few days of taking ill? Look at me, it's been almost two years and I can't get out of my own way."

"Don't be so hard on yourself, Hol."

Holly gave him a smile. "I'm glad everything is okay between us. I wouldn't want to lose you as a friend."

He thought sourly that that's all he could be for her: just a friend. She had a boyfriend but he wondered how serious it was as he'd never seen him around. This Fernando was one mysterious dude. Maybe it was just a casual relationship although Holly hardly seemed the type.

He was distracted by Kenny and Tina putting on their coats. "We're thinking of going someplace else," Tina said.

Jeff and Holly stood next to each other and stared at them.

"Oh, okay, really?" Holly said.

"I thought we were all going to stay in tonight?" Jeff asked, confused. "Now you want to go out?"

"Actually, Tina and I were thinking of going someplace a little quieter," Kenny explained. He looked at Tina who smiled and gave him a small, encouraging nod. "Alone. Just the two of us."

Holly reddened. "Oh, all right. Of course."

Jeff made light of it. "You two kids go out and have a good time. But don't stay out too late."

Kenny and Tina thanked Jeff for the dinner, said their goodbyes and disappeared out the front door.

Jeff looked at Holly. "I guess we've just been dumped."

Holly grinned. "So much for an exciting Friday night."

"That's me, Mr. Excitement," Jeff said half apologetically.

They finished the clean-up quietly. While Jeff scrubbed a pan with a scouring pad, Holly wiped down the countertops and the table. She thought Jeff was awfully quiet and she wondered if he was bothered by the fact that Tina and Kenny had taken off. Maybe he was afraid she was going to insult him again. She had a pile of test papers to be corrected at home but she didn't feel like going home tonight. She really wanted some company and more specifically, she wanted Jeff's company. She lingered, looking around his kitchen for something else to clean or wipe down.

"Dinner was delicious," she commented.

"Thanks," he said, drying the pan with a towel.

"It seems like you're expanding your repertoire," she ventured.

He gave her a small smile. "Trying to."

"Are you upset that Tina took off with Kenny?" she asked.

"What? No!" he said. "I think it's great they found each other."

"Oh, it's just that you seem kind of quiet."

"I'm disappointed. It's Friday night and it's not even ten yet and here I am," he said.

"I know how you feel," she said. "So, you have a thing for disaster movies."

"I won't lie. I do."

"Do you have *The Towering Inferno* on DVD?" she asked, nodding toward his television.

"Both DVD and Blu-Ray," he said. When she didn't say anything, he asked with a little uncertainty, "Did you want to watch it?"

She looked up at him, her green eyes ablaze in her face. "I'd love to, if it's not too much trouble."

"No, not at all. Let's do it."

Jeff turned off the light in the kitchen and went to his cabinet of movies. He paused and turned to her. "Although wouldn't you rather watch a Christmas movie?"

"No."

"Because I have *Die Hard*, and that's kind of like a disaster at Christmas."

She laughed and parked herself on the sofa next to Trixie. "Well, maybe we can watch that after *The Towering Inferno*."

CHAPTER FOURTEEN

Holly woke with a start, not recognizing her surroundings, which caused a brief flash of panic. She looked over and saw Jeff, sound asleep in the other corner of his sofa. The dog, Trixie, was also fast asleep, wedged in the middle of the sofa between them. Holly guessed she must have fallen asleep during the second movie. They'd started with *The Towering Inferno*, then afterward they'd made popcorn and Holly had begun to doze off soon after they had started *Die Hard*. She noticed she was covered in a blanket. Jeff must have put that on her. She peered around and glanced at the clock over the stove in the kitchen. It was almost five in the morning but it was pitch black outside. As quietly as she could, she stood up and stretched, and gently placed the blanket over Jeff. He didn't stir. Trixie opened her eyes and watched her, but made no movements. Holly gave her a pat on the head. She picked up the DVD remote and pressed the power button, waiting for the screen to go from blue to black. As she replaced the remote on Jeff's coffee table, his cell phone lit up, with a message flashing across it. It was from someone named Rosemary.

Can't sleep. Thinking about you.

Oh. She froze. She hadn't realized he was seeing someone. She was surprised that it bothered her. She headed out, taking her coat off the chair but not bothering to put it on. She took one last look at Jeff, fast asleep on the couch, and closed the door behind her. Once home, she crawled into bed, pulling the blankets up around her shoulders, feeling groggy. She was surprised how much she had enjoyed herself. Jeff was really funny. He made her laugh, which was something she hadn't done on a regular basis in a long time. It made her feel good—well, maybe not good, but better, and she wanted to feel like that more often. It felt like there was a little glimmer of hope in her life with her new apartment and her new friend. It was no surprise he had a girlfriend. He was a keeper. She just wondered why he hadn't mentioned it to her.

***

When Jeff woke in the morning, he looked around and was disappointed to see that Holly was gone. It had turned into one of the nicest evenings in his recent history. They had gotten all cozied up on the sofa, watching a movie while the snow fell outside the window. She was the most relaxed he had seen her in a long time. She reminded him of the old Holly from years ago, and he was relieved to see that that wonderful girl wasn't totally lost. She was still in there, somewhere.

He picked up his phone off the coffee table and saw the text from Rosemary. After he read it, he frowned, thinking it was a little early in the relationship to be sending each other texts in the middle of the night. But maybe that was just him. Maybe he needed to relax a bit where women were concerned.

Thinking no more of it, he padded upstairs to shower and dress.

***

Rosemary rang Jeff later that morning and asked him if he'd be interested in going to the craft fair. *Why not?* he'd thought. He met her at the community center, outside the candy cane arches that covered the entrance. She was on time and he was relieved she was at least punctual.

"Well, it's nice to see you again." She smiled.

He paid their admission and they strolled around the area looking at the different crafts. He liked Rosemary. She was a nice girl. The smell of cinnamon and clove lingering in the air, and the twinkling Christmas lights that covered just about everything that wasn't moving added a sense of festiveness to the atmosphere. They had lunch at the Gingerbread Café and Jeff thought the conversation flowed easily. He could find nothing wrong with her but something held him back.

She bought some hand-painted Christmas ornaments. Jeff bought one as a gift for his mother. He had never been to the craft fair before. It was an annual event that he had always skipped, but looking around, he realized it was a good way to get your holiday shopping done in one go. He picked up some other crafts, as well: an ornament display shaped like a Christmas tree, and a wreath. Every door should have a wreath, he thought.

A display further on caught his eye. 'Christmas Holly,' it read. His thoughts drifted to the girl next door and the memory of last night. Suddenly, he felt lost in his thoughts and everything, including his date, disappeared from his consciousness.

"Jeff? Jeff?" Rosemary called out.

"Yeah?" he asked.

She laughed. "Where were you there? It was like you had pulled an Elvis and left the building."

"Sorry."

"Anyway, what do you think about this?" she asked, with a laugh. It was a small bag of marshmallows, but it had been labelled 'Snowman Poop.' "I think my nephews would get a kick out of this as a little gag gift."

He laughed to be polite. "That'd be a great gift." He turned his back on the 'Christmas Holly' sign, determined to be more engaged.

***

When he arrived home mid-afternoon, Jeff knocked on Holly's door. He was surprised when she answered it almost immediately. She had her coat on and her purse slung over her shoulder. He was glad he had caught her before she'd gone out.

He gestured with his thumb toward his truck, warming up in his driveway. "I'm heading out to get a Christmas tree—are you sure you don't want one?"

She hesitated. "I can't. I've got to make a run to the grocery store to get groceries for my Christmas dinner." She sounded harried.

"I could pick one up for you," he offered.

"No, please don't do that," she said firmly.

"Oh, okay," he said. He wondered what had happened since last night when they fell asleep watching movies. She had let her guard down but today she was back to her cautious, hesitant self.

"Thanks anyway," she said.

"Is everything all right?" he asked.

"Yes, of course," she said a little too shrilly.

He turned to walk away but she called out to him. He turned around to look at her, something clutching in his heart once again. What was it about her that made his insides do somersaults?

"I know we talked about going together to the benefit tomorrow, but I understand if you'd rather give the ticket to someone else," she said.

He frowned, wondering why she would think he'd want to do that. Who else would he give it to?

"I assumed we were still going together. Doesn't make sense for us to drive two cars." His heart started to beat quickly as he began to jump to all the wrong conclusions and label the event as a date with Holly. That was dangerous thinking. And no good would come of it.

She nodded. "If you don't mind."

His mind raced with all sorts of imagined scenarios involving his pretty neighbor. He really had to stop doing that, he told himself. He was only setting himself up for disappointment. She closed the door. Jeff climbed into his truck. He had found a Christmas tree farm online where you picked out a tree and cut it down yourself. For years, he'd depended on his artificial tabletop tree, but this Christmas, he wanted to do something different. Something bigger. Something better. He was alive and there was an amazing girl living next door and if that didn't warrant a real Christmas tree, he didn't know what did.

***

Luckily it had been pretty busy at the diner Sunday morning, with a steady stream of customers, so the time flew for Holly and before she knew it, it was time to go home. Sylvia had graciously agreed to let her leave by noon so she could go home and get ready for the spaghetti dinner. Customers were generally in a festive mood and this was reflected in her bulging tip bag. She clocked out promptly at twelve, anxious to get home, shower off the smell of frying oil and get ready for her evening with Jeff at the annual fireman's Christmas dinner. She didn't know what she was looking forward to more: the event itself and the difference it would make for the Sanders family, or spending the evening with Jeff.

She put on her hat, tucking her curls up into it. She pulled up the collar of her coat, wound her scarf around her neck, and said goodnight to the rest of the girls. She stopped at the front door to dig through her purse for her car keys when something—or rather someone—caught her eye. The hostess was leading a family to a booth on the opposite side of the restaurant near the window, a younger couple with a baby, accompanied by an older couple, presumably the grandparents. Holly slowly made her way to the glass doors at the front, a hollow feeling settling in her stomach. When the younger man turned around and slid into the booth, she froze to the spot and swallowed hard.

Tim.

CHAPTER FIFTEEN

Holly stood there at the front entrance of the Olympic, unable to move for what seemed like an eternity. She hadn't seen Tim in two years. She had tried for six months to locate him, to no avail. As unobtrusively as possible, she studied him. The petite blonde who was with him held a baby in her arms. A girl, judging by the pink snowsuit, no more than five or six months old. The older couple must be the woman's parents. Holly stared, still unbelieving. Same old Tim: long, square jaw and that cowlick in the front of his blonde hair. Her immediate knee-jerk reaction was to march over to his booth and confront him, but she decided against that. She didn't want to make a scene in a public place and air her dirty laundry. Besides, she'd have to return to the restaurant for work, and then everyone would know her business. She also didn't trust Tim to give her his contact details. He had done nothing in the past two years to get in touch with her and pay his share of the court-ordered repayment plan. He had disappeared for a reason. He hadn't wanted to be found. He was making cooing sounds to the baby and a sick feeling took hold in Holly's stomach. Luckily, he hadn't noticed her so she stepped into the outer vestibule, out of sight. She gathered her thoughts and slowly walked out of the restaurant, going around the long way to the parking lot out back so Tim wouldn't catch sight of her out the window as she walked by.

She sat in her car, started the ignition and waited for the heat to kick in. She decided she'd wait for Tim to come out and then follow him home. She looked at her watch. She was never going to get home in time to go to that dinner with Jeff. But right now, this was more important. Quickly, she tapped out a text to Jeff letting him know she'd got caught up and wouldn't be able to join him. She knew it was lame but she had no other choice. She'd explain it to Jeff later. She knew he'd understand.

She drove around to the front of the building and reversed into a spot directly across from the entrance. She'd wait there all night for Tim to come out if she had to. But she suspected that at some point they would have to get that little baby home to bed. He would never recognize her ten-year-old junker. She had had to sell her newer-model car to pay off debts after he'd disappeared.

***

Jeff sat on his couch in his suit and tie, ready to go, listening for the sound of Holly's car pulling into the driveway next door. Trixie was curled up in the corner of the sofa next to him. He was determined to have a good time—how could he not with Holly there? He hoped there would be a good turnout. Mrs. Hopkins, one of the classroom mothers, had organized a holiday gift auction in conjunction with the spaghetti dinner with all proceeds going to the Sanders family. Jeff's mother and Morty were going. His neighbors, Stan and Mrs. Peters, had also promised they would attend. Stan had even hinted at a possible appearance by the elusive Gladys. Jeff just hoped Mrs. Peters wouldn't bring Trudy. He shuddered at that thought.

He kept glancing at his watch, wondering what was keeping Holly. She should have been home by now. His cell phone beeped and Jeff picked it up and stared at the text.

Held up at work. Go on without me. Sorry. Holly x

"Just terrific," he muttered, and tossed his phone on the coffee table. For a brief moment, he thought of not going himself. All of a sudden he had lost interest, but then he remembered two things: the promise he'd made to the fire chief and the fact that this was for the Sanders family. The old Jeff would have curled up into a ball, turned on the television and ordered a pizza. But not the new Jeff. He jumped up from the sofa so fast that even Trixie raised her head.

"It's all right, Trix," Jeff reassured her. The dog laid her head back down but did not close her eyes, keeping a watch on Jeff.

Jeff grabbed his coat and keys and headed out the door.

**

It was an hour before Tim, the woman, the baby and the older couple emerged from the restaurant. Tim looked so happy Holly wanted to punch him in the face. Where had he been all this time? It was obvious—making babies! She wondered what he had told the current woman he was with. Apparently, whatever it was, she had believed it, as evidenced by their little bundle of joy. An ache invaded Holly's heart: this woman was living the life she had once dreamed of.

Gritting her teeth, she threw her car into drive. Her fingers were practically numb. They were parked directly in front of her. A brand-new SUV. *Must be nice,* Holly thought. She watched with a mixture of envy, fury and sadness as Tim took the beautiful baby from the woman and strapped her carefully into the carrier in the back seat. He climbed into the driver's seat and started the car. There was a big Rudolph nose attached to the front grill of the car. The older couple got into a luxury sedan parked next to Tim's SUV. They were one big, happy family.

When Tim pulled out, he was engaged in an animated conversation with the woman. Holly didn't even think he noticed her rowing in behind him. From the parking lot, he turned right. Holly stayed close; she didn't care. Within five miles, he turned left and then a quick right into a housing development. There was a big brick sign that read, 'Shady Oaks.' That was an adjective that definitely applied to Tim. She peered through the windshield at the stately stone and brick homes. She swallowed her anger. Could Tim have been hiding out here these last two years while she'd been scraping to get by and working a second job? If so, she would surely go into orbit. How could he afford to live here?

Soon, he pulled into a wide driveway behind the car of the older couple. It was a two-story red brick home with black shutters. Holly slowed down so she could get a better look at the sprawling home. Two big wreaths with festive red ribbons festooned the double front doors. The garage door opened and Holly saw a navy BMW sedan parked to one side. The first car pulled into the garage and Tim parked the SUV in the driveway. The woman took the baby into the house while Tim opened the back of the SUV and pulled out shopping bags from the rear of the car.

Holly drove slowly to the end of the street and turned around. As she swung by the house for a second look, the garage door was coming back down and Holly parked the car directly across the street. She grabbed a piece of paper and pen from her purse and wrote down the address. Not that she would forget it. She studied the house long and hard, committing it to memory. She thought for a while and decided now wasn't the time for a confrontation. Oh, she was going to confront Tim, all right, but she wanted everything to be well thought-out. She started the car and headed home, thinking of a plan.

CHAPTER SIXTEEN

The firehall that adjoined the firehouse was the venue for the dinner and the holiday gift auction to benefit the Sanders family. Avoiding the parking lot, Jeff drove down to the end of the street and parked there, deciding to walk it, even though it was bitter cold outside.

As soon as he went inside, he was greeted with bright lights and noise. He took a deep breath and walked right into all the commotion. He tried not to think about Holly and how disappointed he was that she had stiffed him at the last moment. But as hard as he tried, it was all he could think about. He wondered what had happened to cause her to bail. It was unlike her. Maybe she'd had second thoughts about going with him.

The doors hadn't opened yet to the general public but there was a jolly buzz among the volunteers. He headed toward the big commercial kitchen. It was hot and full of men and women from the fire department manning the big cauldrons of spaghetti and sauce. He saw Martha McHenry slicing up loaves of garlic bread.

"Hey Martha, do you need some help?"

She looked around the crowded kitchen. "Actually, Jeff, I think we've got too many people in here. Sorry."

"Not a problem, let me know if you need anything."

He headed back out to the main hall looking for something to do or someone to help.

He quickly wigged on to the fact that Mrs. Hopkins was the short woman with the brutally blunt haircut. She was issuing directions and commands to those around her like a general going into battle. He supposed he should introduce himself and get his own marching orders. He was intercepted by Kenny and Tina.

"Hey," Kenny said by way of greeting. He was holding Tina's hand. She looked at Kenny with a look that was just for him. Jeff felt a pang of envy.

"Hey yourself, I just got here," Jeff said.

Tina frowned. "Where's Holly?"

Jeff tried to sound casual as he shrugged. "I don't know. She sent me a text and told me she couldn't make it."

"Really? Where else would she be? I mean, this is all she's been talking about for the last two weeks, helping this girl in her class and her family."

"Look, I don't know where she is. I'm not her keeper." Jeff walked away but not before he caught Kenny and Tina exchange a glance. He went in search of Mrs. Hopkins and a task he could do to keep himself busy and distracted, and his mind off the no-show, Holly.

***

Holly began to formulate a plan for confronting Tim on the way home. She had always felt there would be some sort of jubilation in finding him. But oddly, there had been no joy in seeing him or even in knowing his whereabouts. It had only served to remove a scab from a wound she wanted healed. She had assumed he had left the country—she had pictured him on some sunny beach in the Caribbean, sipping tropical drinks—and instead here he was on the other side of Bluff Falls, changing diapers in a house with expensive wreaths and a double garage.

The baby had thrown her for a loop. Of all the imagined scenarios, she had not expected to find him with a ready-made family. When they'd been together, they had talked about starting a family but he'd seemed ambivalent. She'd chalked it up to long hours at work and his focus on his career. She had been excited about the prospect of becoming a mother once they were married but he had told her they would need to wait at least two years, until they were in a better financial position. And she had believed him. Looking back, she could see they had been in a great financial position. And now, here he was with a brand-new partner and a brand-new baby.

She pulled into her driveway and noticed Jeff's truck wasn't parked out front. He must have gone on to the benefit. He had never replied to her text. She hoped he wasn't mad at her. Once inside, she glanced at the clock and decided she had to get a move on and get ready and get to the benefit. The dinner was most likely over but she could be there for the gift auction. She really didn't want to miss it. It was too important. And what would it say to the Sanders family, and Grace especially, if her very own teacher didn't bother to show up? She took a quick shower and pulled her green velvet dress from her closet, the one she liked to wear around the holidays. She put on some makeup and did her hair and managed to get out of the house within forty minutes. She bundled up in her good winter coat and headed out the door, getting excited about the benefit.

***

Jeff saw Holly come through the doors of the firehall. She was slightly breathless and the cold night air had given her cheeks a pinkish glow. Her hair tumbled in loose curls to her shoulders. She wore a green dress and Jeff thought she was the prettiest girl he'd seen in a long time. Why on earth had he allowed himself to get his hopes up with Holly? How could he let himself fall into the trap of thinking she was different? He noticed she was coming in his direction. He made himself busy. There had been a great turnout, better than expected. It looked to him like everyone from Bluff Falls had made it their business to show up that afternoon. He had seen Trudy with Mrs. Peters and had spent the afternoon knowing where she was at all times so he could be on the other side of the room. They actually had run out of spaghetti at one point and someone had to make a run to the grocery store for another ten pounds of pasta. The dinner was just finishing and the clean-up had commenced. He was clearing plates from the table and carrying them back to the kitchen.

Earlier, he had strolled around the tables showcasing the auction. There were incredible items up for bid: there was a four-day cruise; there were spa baskets; there was an electric fence for a dog, although he personally didn't bother with that one as he had no fear of Trixie ever running off. She just didn't have it in her. There was a free appointment for will and estate planning. He wasn't going to worry about that, either. The one he'd really like to win was the year-long membership to the local gym. He'd dumped half of his tickets into that one. The rest of his tickets he'd put into the pot for one of six Fitbits donated by Calvin & Sons Insurance Agency. Holly was still coming in his direction so he pretended not to see her and turned so his back was to her. As he did, he came face to face with a couple in disco garb.

"Ma, is that you?" he asked, blinking in disbelief at the hot pants, the white go-go boots and the psychedelic sash wrapped around her wig of long blonde curly hair.

"It sure is, what do you think, honey?" she asked.

"Where are your clothes?" he asked, looking around to see if people were staring. He looked at Morty and his eyes widened. His mother's boyfriend was sporting a black afro wig, a white leisure suit and platform shoes. His shirt was unbuttoned, revealing a few heavy gold chains against a mat of gray chest hair. It was a sight Jeff was sure would haunt his dreams in the foreseeable future.

"What the hell happened to you?" Jeff asked.

Morty laughed. "Hey, don't knock it, this was how we dressed way back when."

"Maybe you should have left it in the way back when," Jeff observed.

"What's the matter, honey? You seem a little surly," Ginger asked, concern flooding her face beneath her glittery make-up.

"I'm fine, Ma," Jeff said abruptly.

"Where's Holly?" she asked.

"I don't know," he lied.

"Oh wait, there she is! Holly! Holly!" Ginger waved.

"Ma, stop it, you're drawing attention to yourself," Jeff hissed.

"What is wrong with you tonight?" she demanded.

"Nothing," he muttered.

"Oh, here she comes. Come on, Morty, let's skedaddle," Ginger said, taking Morty's hand and leading him away.

***

"Hey, Jeff," Holly said, tapping him on the shoulder. She'd seen him from across the room. She'd thought he looked so handsome in his shirt and tie. His shirtsleeves were rolled up revealing muscular arms. He was busy clearing plates from a table.

He turned around and gave her a brief smile. "Oh, Holly. Nice of you to come."

There was a bit of an edge to his voice and Holly was briefly taken aback.

"I'm sorry for being late—" she started, but he cut her off.

"It's no skin off my back," he said tersely. "It's not like it was a date or something."

"No...I guess it wasn't," she said slowly, feeling disappointed. "But if you'd let me explain—"

"You don't need to justify it to me."

She felt her anger begin to well up. She couldn't understand why he was acting like a spoiled brat. This just wasn't Jeff. "I'm not justifying it. There's nothing to justify. I'm trying to explain why I got held up." Suddenly she felt tired, and she no longer cared to explain it to him.

"Like I said, it's none of my business," Jeff said. He looked around as if he'd rather be anywhere else but there. "Besides, maybe I'm tired of being Mr. Nice Guy to everybody. It gets me absolutely nowhere."

With a stack of dirty dishes in his hands, he turned to walk away but Holly grabbed hold of his arm. "Wait a minute. Where is this coming from? Do you really think I would just blow you off at the last minute without a good reason?"

He said without smiling, "Well the thing is, I really wouldn't know. I haven't known you for that long. You're just my tenant."

Holly flinched. She was speechless for only a moment but quickly regained her composure and said evenly, "Thank you for reminding me." She tilted her head to the side and added, "I hope you have a nice evening."

She turned on her heel, trying to control the shaky feeling that pervaded her body. She clamped her teeth together to stop the flow of tears. Her cheeks burned. She caught Tina waving and she forced a smile onto her face as she headed in the direction of her best friend, determined to have a good time.

As soon as he'd called Holly his 'tenant' and saw the expression on her face, Jeff had wanted to die. What had come over him? Had he lost his mind? He shook his head. No wonder he was alone. There really was no hope for him. He'd had a gut feeling about Holly the moment he met her all those years ago, and he trusted his gut. Holly was good people. She must have had a good reason for being late. It was his fear that had lashed out at her. He had assigned way too many hopes to this evening and inevitably set himself up for a fall. He felt sick. He carried the plates to the kitchen and returned to get more, determined to stay busy.

Stan intercepted him as he exited the kitchen.

"There you are, Jeff!" exclaimed Stan, slapping him on the back. "I want you to meet Gladys."

"Oh sure," Jeff said, not paying attention. He turned around to catch sight of Stan but it was the woman next to him that caused Jeff to stop in his tracks. However he had pictured Stan's new love interest, this wasn't it. He had assumed she'd be short with a blue rinse and glasses. Not the real Gladys—she was as far from that image as possible. She was a big woman, taller than both Jeff and Stan, and she wore her white hair in a bun on top of her head, adding a few more inches to her stature, which Jeff guessed to be about six foot four. He was no stylist but he thought she might want to avoid any hairstyles piled on top of her head. Then he gave himself a mental shake—she could wear her hair any way she damn well pleased. What business was it of his? She wore a pair of black slacks with a red turtleneck and a heavy Christmas sweater adorned with reindeer. Her brown eyes twinkled in her face. Jeff looked back to Stan, who was clearly besotted, judging by the way he gazed at her.

"Well, Gladys, it's nice to meet you," Jeff said. "I've heard a lot about you. All good, I can assure you." He assessed her, thinking if he ever got involved in tag-team mixed martial arts, he wanted Gladys as his backup.

She raised her eyebrows. "And I've heard a lot about *you*." Her mirthful voice had a deep, rich timber.

"I can just imagine." Jeff shot a glance at Stan, who smiled innocently and shrugged. "Are you two kids having fun?"

"We are. They've got some great things for the auction," Gladys answered.

"We put all our tickets in for the jacuzzi," Stan enthused. He wrapped his arm around his date and gave a little squeeze. Jeff tried not to draw up a mental image of the two of them in a hot tub together but it was just about impossible.

"Well, then I guess I'm glad Stan lives across the street and not behind me," Jeff cracked.

Gladys guffawed and slapped his arm so hard Jeff momentarily feared she might have broken it.

"Didn't I tell you, Gladys, that he was a real card?" Stan said.

"You did indeed, Stan," Gladys said.

"I thought I saw Holly earlier," Stan said, "But haven't seen her since. I thought she'd be with you."

"Why?" Jeff asked and he hated that he sounded like a little kid who had had too much sugar and stayed way too late at the party.

Stan shrugged again. "I don't know. It just seems like lately, I haven't seen one of you without the other."

Gladys chimed in. "Yes, even Mrs. Peters said the two of you were becoming fast friends."

He thought bitterly about how that friendship had just crashed and burned, and he had been the one responsible for throwing lighter fluid and a match on it.

He tried to sound vague and gave a glance around. "I'm sure she's around here somewhere. One of the Sanders kids is in her class." He knew very well where Holly was. She had parked herself at a table with Tina and Kenny. She had probably told them all about his bad behavior. He couldn't blame her. He had taken great care to avoid that side of the hall and had focused on clearing the tables on the opposite side.

"Well, Jeff, we'll leave you to it," Stan said. "I just wanted you to meet Gladys."

Jeff nodded and watched as the two octogenarian lovebirds disappeared into the crowd. Well, Stan disappeared. Gladys was head and shoulders above everyone else.

He glanced around, seeing that for the most part, the tables were cleared. It was after four, the auction would be starting soon. He grabbed himself a light beer and stood there in the thick of the crowd, alone.

There was a loud screech and all eyes turned to the podium, where Mrs. Hopkins stood, trying to adjust the microphone. She winced as the sound reverberated through the hall.

"Sorry about that." She smiled apologetically. She brushed back her bangs with her hand and waited for it to quiet down in the hall. "I just want to thank everyone here for coming out tonight, despite the cold weather, to support the Sanders family. My name is Sherry Hopkins and I was honored to be asked to help with this event. A big, big thank you to the Bluff Falls Fire Department for graciously letting us use their firehall for the venue, and for donating all the proceeds from this dinner to the Sanders family. Every little bit will help the family get back on their feet and rebuild their lives. I'd ask that you get your tickets out as we're going to start the auction. One last thing before we start: I want to wish each and every one of you a very merry Christmas!"

The hall erupted in clapping and shouts. She strode toward the first of the prize tables. At that moment, the Sanders kids appeared and everyone in the hall stood up and clapped for them. They were going to do the picking of the winners. All three of them, Grace, Harry and Ben, were all dressed up and smiled shyly for everyone. Jeff thought they were a great looking family. Suddenly, he felt an ache in his chest that had nothing to do with his previous cardiac problems. He would give anything to have a family of his own. His eyes strayed toward Holly. He didn't want her to be just his tenant, that's what had made him so angry earlier.

Grace Sanders pulled out a ticket from the white bucket in front of the spa package prize. Mrs. Hopkins called out the number and then repeated it, the sounds in the firehall quieting to a murmur as everyone checked their tickets. Suddenly, there was a squeal at the table behind Jeff that almost gave him a real heart attack—apparently someone there held the winning ticket.

"They're not going to scream like that every time someone wins something? That's unacceptable." It was the voice of Alan Fulbright. Jeff turned around and pasted a smile on his face as Holly's parents emerged from the crowd to stand beside him.

"Jeff, how are you?" Gloria asked.

He nodded. "Fine. Thanks for coming."

"Where's my daughter?" Alan asked.

How should I know? Jeff thought. He shrugged and said, "She's around here somewhere."

Mrs. Hopkins moved along the prize table to the second item. This time it was Harry who pulled a raffle ticket out of the bucket, and Mrs. Hopkins proceeded to call out the number.

"Mrs. Fulbright, can I ask a favor? Can you look after my tickets?" Jeff asked.

She nodded and took his auction tickets from him. He thanked her and clapped Mr. Fulbright on the shoulder.

Jeff made his way across the hall to where he had last seen Holly, at a table with Tina and Kenny. He had it all planned out in his head. He was going to ask to speak to her alone and then he was going to do the right thing: apologize. He was going to tell her that he had had a momentary bout of insanity and ask for her forgiveness. He was halfway there, when Martha stopped him. "Hey, can you give us a hand in the kitchen? The dirty dishes are piling up and the last dishwasher went out for a smoke and hasn't returned."

Jeff was torn. He could see Holly at the table with Kenny and Tina and all he wanted to do was talk to her. To apologize. But he couldn't refuse a request for assistance. He'd have to talk to Holly later.

"No problem, Martha," he said and followed her back into the kitchen.

The previous crowd that had been in the kitchen earlier preparing the dinner had thinned considerably. Jeff looked at the piles of plates stacked high on the industrial sink and was disheartened.

"Come on, Kowalek," Martha smiled. "You wash and I'll dry."

He nodded and headed toward the sink and the task, determined to finish it quickly so he could go talk to Holly.

***

Holly watched Jeff approach her table but then turn around and follow another woman into the kitchen. She was disappointed. She had hoped he was coming over to join them. His behavior earlier was so unlike him she was wondering what was up. Tina had managed to save her a plate of spaghetti and Holly had wolfed it down, unaware of how ravenous she was. As she ate, she told Tina and Kenny about her sighting of Tim earlier that day. They sat there, shocked and offered her support.

After the auction, she spoke briefly to Mr. and Mrs. Sanders who were clearly overcome with the outpouring of support from the community. Then she sought out her student, Grace.

Grace looked lovely in navy blue taffeta dress with a wide sash.

Holly greeted her. "Grace, how are you doing?"

The young girl, nodded, smiling. "I'm good."

"I'm glad to hear that."

"I'm having a lot of fun. It was fun picking out the lucky numbers, although my mother said we couldn't enter any tickets in the raffle."

"That must have been disappointing," Holly said.

"No, not really," Grace said. "Besides, I've got this." She opened her hand to reveal two twenty dollar bills.

Holly's eyes widened. "Oh, where did you get those?"

Grace turned, scanning the crowd. "I don't see her, but she had a belt around her hair and she was wearing a funny outfit."

Holly laughed. That description could only be Mrs. Kowalek who had left with Morty to go to her disco party.

And then Grace turned and looked behind Holly. "And that man back there, with the white hair and red sweater?"

Holly's eyes landed on her father.

Grace continued, "They each gave me twenty dollars and told me to buy what I want."

"And what will you buy?" Holly asked, smiling and already knowing the answer.

Grace grinned. "Books!"

***

Jeff rinsed out the sink when he was finished and washed his hands. He rolled down his shirt sleeves and put his tie back on. He grabbed his suit jacket off the back of the chair in the kitchen and headed out to find Holly. The auction was over and the crowd had diminished. He headed toward Kenny and Tina's table where he last saw Holly. His heart sank when he reached the table to see that Holly was gone.

"Hey, what's up, buddy," Kenny said, with his arm around Tina's shoulder.

"Not much, how are you guys?" he asked. He pulled up the chair next to Kenny. "Have you seen Holly?"

"You just missed her," Tina said. "She's gone home."

"Did she tell you what happened today?" Kenny asked.

Jeff shook his head. "No, we really didn't talk much this afternoon."

Tina chimed in. "She's getting ready to leave work this afternoon and who walks into the restaurant but Tim, her deadbeat ex-fiancé."

"You're kidding," Jeff said. A sick feeling was beginning to form in his stomach. He hadn't given her a chance to explain and she had had a valid reason for being late. He wished he could kick himself right in the pants.

"She follows him home," Kenny explained. "And get this—the jerk has moved on. He's got a new wife and a baby!"

"No!" Jeff said, appalled. He felt so sorry for Holly. And she would have explained all this to him if he had just let her. He truly didn't deserve her forgiveness or her friendship. But he could try. He stood up. "I've got to go. I'll talk to you later."

He stopped. "Wait—did Holly say anything to you about me?"

Tina looked at him blankly and Kenny frowned. "Say anything about you? What is this? At the lockers in high school?"

"Jeff, why don't you just tell her how you feel?" Tina suggested.

Mortified, Jeff left the two of them at the table and went out into the frosty night.

CHAPTER SEVENTEEN

Holly came downstairs after a hot bath and was glad to be in her pajamas and bathrobe. She looked around the dark apartment at her few personal Christmas decorations. She promised herself there would a little bit more next year. Maybe even a tree. She flipped on the overhead light in the kitchen and a lamp in the living room to dispel the shadows. She turned her kettle on and pulled down a tin of cocoa and her favorite mug. She spooned the chocolatey powder into her cup and thought about Jeff. Tears blurred her vision as she thought of how angry he'd been. She had thought they were friends and if she allowed herself to admit it, she'd begun to hope it might develop into something more. But he had made it clear tonight that he thought of her strictly as a tenant. She couldn't blame him. Jeff Kowalek was a nice guy, but just because he was nice didn't mean she could—or should—expect him to take on her and her sad, sorry tale. He deserved much better than she could offer him. Why would any man take her on with all her baggage: a hefty court-ordered repayment plan and bad credit to boot? She, Holly Fulbright, definitely wasn't for the faint of heart. The kettle whistled and she poured the boiling water into the mug and gave it a good stir. Splurging, she topped it off with a bit of canned whipped cream. She heard a noise outside and went to the front window, where she saw Jeff pulling into his driveway. He killed his headlights and got out of his truck. She hoped and prayed he would knock on her door. Quickly, she ducked out of view—she didn't want him to see her standing there, thinking she was spying on him. She backtracked into the kitchen and realized she needed to feed Fernando. She called him several times and only when she opened the can of cat food with the electric can opener did she see him darting down the staircase. Once the cat was fed, she leaned against the counter, sipping her cocoa. She waited, hoping Jeff would come to her front door. She listened for the sound of a knock or the doorbell ringing, but it never came.

***

When Jeff pulled into the driveway, he saw lights on in Holly's house and decided he was going to march over there and apologize and quite possibly, if the spirit moved him, declare his feelings for her. He trotted up the steps and crossed their common porch. As he passed her front window, he could hear her calling out for Fernando. He stopped in his tracks. He had hoped Holly's Latin lover was out of the picture, but apparently that wasn't the case. There was no way he was going to apologize with him there. Even Jeff Kowalek had his pride. He sighed. This just wasn't working out. He looked up and down the street. Every house was awash in bright lights of red, orange, blue and white for Christmas, and yet the sight made him feel melancholy. He just didn't want to be alone anymore, at Christmas or at any time of the year.

***

There was a knock on Holly's front door early the next morning as she ate her bowl of cornflakes. She pulled her bathrobe more tightly around her and answered the door to find Jeff standing on her porch.

"Hi Jeff," she said. She couldn't help but notice the discomfort on his face. She opened the door wider and invited him in.

He followed her into the kitchen and joined her at the table when she motioned him into a chair. She felt embarrassed about their previous encounter and couldn't look him in the eye. To lighten the mood, she said, "Can I interest you in a bowl of corn flakes?"

He shook his head. "No, thanks. Just had my breakfast."

Holly reached for her purse on the counter and began to rifle through it. She pulled out a small box and handed it to Jeff.

"My mother gave me that to give to you. You won it in the auction yesterday."

Jeff smiled at the Fitbit. "That's great, thanks." He turned the box over in his hand and studied it. There was a brief silence and she waited. She didn't know what to say.

Jeff set the box down on the table and folded his hands and stared at them. He finally spoke without looking at her. "Actually, I came over to apologize. Yesterday afternoon at the dinner, my behavior was appalling."

"It's okay," she said.

He finally looked up at her. "No, Holly, it isn't. I had no right to talk to you like that."

She smiled, relieved. "Apology accepted."

He looked down at his hands again. "I want you to know that you are more than a tenant to me. Much more."

She held her breath and looked at him expectantly. He continued, "You've become a very good friend to me and I value our friendship too much to ever jeopardize it."

She deflated. There it was. Friends. She felt herself begin to shake, surprised at the depth of her own disappointment. Only then, in that moment, did she realize her true feelings for Jeff Kowalek.

"Are you all right?" he asked, studying her.

She straightened abruptly, trying to cover up her feelings. "Yes, I'm fine. Our friendship means a lot to me, too."

There was another lengthy silence and a feeling in the air that something had come and gone and passed, that whatever had been possible for her and Jeff was no longer. Just when she was starting to come up for air in her life, this threatened to pull her back under.

"Tina told me you ran into your ex yesterday," Jeff said quietly.

"Oh yeah," she said. "And by all accounts, he appears to be doing well."

"What are you going to do?" he asked.

"I've been thinking about that. I'm going to confront him, but I want to prepare."

"Good idea," Jeff said. "But promise me one thing."

She waited for him to go on.

"Don't go out there alone," he entreated. "Take someone with you for backup."

She smiled to herself. He might not be interested in her romantically but he did care about her. There was some comfort in that.

"Why, did you want to go with me?" she asked.

"Me?" he repeated. She immediately regretted asking him.

"Sorry, of course, I didn't mean to drag you into this mess," she said, her cheeks burning.

"No, no, it's not that at all. Of course I'd go with you, but what about Fernando?"

Holly looked at Jeff, confused. "Fernando? What about him?"

Now it was Jeff's turn to look confused. "Well, I know the two of you, uh, spend time together, so I just thought..." His voice trailed off.

She answered slowly, staring at him. "Of course we spend time together—he lives here. But why in the world would I take him with me to see Tim?"

"Wait—he *lives* here? How come I never see him around?" Jeff asked in disbelief.

"Because that's just the way he is," she said, wondering about the bizarre turn their conversation had taken.

"I never see him coming or going," Jeff persisted.

"Probably because he doesn't go outside," Holly explained.

Jeff narrowed his eyes at her. "You didn't say on the lease that he'd be living with you."

Holly felt all flustered. They were back to the tenant thing again. "I asked your mother when she showed me the place if it was okay if I brought him, and she said it would be fine, that you'd have no problem with it." She didn't understand why Jeff was so upset; she knew there were landlords out there who said absolutely no pets, but Jeff had a dog himself.

"I wouldn't if he didn't sound even more weird than me. Look, I hate to pull rank, but as your landlord, I have a right to know who's living in my house."

"Of course," she agreed quickly. She began to panic. What if she was forced to give up Fernando? He had been the only thing that had kept her sane the last two years. She'd have to move all over again. She didn't think she could do it. And where would she find a new apartment so close to Christmas? Impossible.

Jeff stood and folded his arms across his chest and said stiffly, "Holly, if it's not too much trouble, I'd like to meet Fernando."

She thought it was odd but after all, he was the landlord. She blinked and pulled herself together. "Sure."

"I appreciate that."

"Fernando can be fussy," she warned. "He may not want to come out."

"Well, tell him the landlord insists on meeting him," Jeff said.

Holly giggled. "He probably won't care that you're the landlord." When Jeff didn't even crack a smile, she stopped laughing. She couldn't understand why he was acting so strange.

She started calling out, "Fernando! Fernando?" She turned back to Jeff. "He's probably gone back to the bedroom. It's his favorite place—can't get him out of it," Holly said.

"I bet," Jeff said tightly.

Hurriedly, she ran up the stairs, her anxiety skyrocketing. Why on earth would Jeff be upset over a cat? "Fernando!" Holly called. She disappeared into her bedroom and found the cat sound asleep on the middle of the bed. She pulled him to her, loving the feel of the soft, furry animal. "There you are, silly, I've been calling you," she whispered. "The landlord wants to meet you. Although why, I don't know."

With her cat cradled in her arms, Holly marched down the stairs and brought Fernando out to meet Jeff. Jeff turned around and the expression on his face changed to one of complete shock.

"Jeff, I'd like you to meet Fernando," she said. "Fernando is six—"

Before she could finish, Jeff started laughing and couldn't stop. He laughed so hard he was bent over at the waist. Holly stared at him as if he had lost his mind. He straightened up and Holly saw that his face was beet red and tears streamed down his face. He took in a deep breath, steadied himself, tried to say something, and then started laughing again. Holly didn't know what was so funny. Fernando was a lovely cat: a black and gray striped beauty, perfectly formed. She was beginning to get aggravated. She also began to worry about Jeff's volatile state of mind.

"Do you mind sharing with me what's so funny?" she asked. She held her cat closer to her.

Jeff hooted a few more times, wiped his eyes and began to settle down. Once he caught his breath, he said, "I didn't know Fernando was a cat."

Holly looked at him, not comprehending.

Jeff gave a short bark of laughter. "I thought he was your boyfriend."

"You did not!" she protested.

He nodded. "Oh, I did!"

"How could you have thought that?" she asked.

"Apparently, very easily," he said. He coughed, blinking back tears. "I'm so sorry, Holly."

Holly found herself laughing, too. "So, Fernando can stay?" she asked.

He nodded again. "Of course. He's more than welcome."

Holly chuckled as she replayed their conversation in her mind.

"Every time you mentioned Fernando, I was picturing some Latin American beefcake," Jeff explained, struggling to keep his voice even.

Holly blushed. "Oh, Jeff." She smiled, shaking her head.

They both fell silent, stared at each other, then dissolved into laughter again.

CHAPTER EIGHTEEN

On Monday night, Jeff pulled into the parking lot of the retail toy store. He and Holly had volunteered for the task of shopping for the Sanders children for Christmas with some of the proceeds from the benefit. So much had been raised at the charity dinner that it had been decided a portion would go toward toys and clothes for each child, as well as a laptop for the family to share. The remainder of the money would be given to Mr. and Mrs. Sanders to spend as they saw fit. The proceeds could never replace the sentimental items that had been destroyed like photo albums, furniture that had been lovingly handed down or favorite toys from when the kids were babies, but everyone in Bluff Falls hoped the Sanders family would be buoyed by the outreach and the support of the community.

Jeff, with Holly in the passenger seat beside him, cruised to the front of the lot and was elated when he spotted the open space next to the handicap spot. But then he looked at the Fitbit strapped to his wrist. He decided he better forfeit the spot nearest to the door. He looked forlornly at the vacant parking spot right in front of the building and said to Holly, "Do you mind if we park farther away? I'm trying to get some exercise."

Holly looked at him and smiled and he tried not to melt. "Not at all. In fact, park behind the building if you prefer," she suggested brightly.

He let out a nervous laugh. "Let's not get carried away, now."

He parked the truck at the end of a long row of cars. The thick, wet snow that had recently covered the parking lot had already turned gray. He and Holly made their way to the front entrance, stamping their feet free of slush on the charcoal winter mat.

"I suppose we'll need two carts," Jeff said.

"Most likely," she agreed.

As Jeff freed two carts from the corral, Holly pulled the lists from her purse. Mrs. Sanders had provided her with a list for each of her children. Each child had written down three things they truly wanted and then their mother had added what each child's interests were, along with their clothing sizes.

Holly unfolded the three lists. Grace's was on top. Under her list of three favorite things, she had written 'books, books, books.' Holly laughed. She would have expected nothing else.

"What's so funny?" Jeff asked.

"Grace," Holly looked up from the list. "All she wants are books."

Jeff smiled. "That's easy. I guess we'll be stopping by the bookstore later."

Holly nodded and scanned the rest of her list. "She also has an interest in science and history."

"Good for her," Jeff said.

Holly handed Jeff the girl's list, then looked at Harry's and Ben's.

She read aloud: "Harry, aged seven, is interested in any kind of sport and wants a soccer net for Christmas with the accompanying gear."

Jeff read from the final list. "Ben, aged four, loves dinosaurs and doing various arts and crafts. He wants a T-rex from Santa." He added, "Hopefully, not a real one. He also wants a scooter."

They started with Ben first and found themselves in the aisle for his age group. Both Holly and Jeff were quickly overwhelmed by the vast selection of toys. They decided to head over to the sports section for Harry. They both became immersed in checking out the toys and games and soon realized an hour had passed without them making any decisions. They agreed to split up. Jeff would concentrate on the boys and Holly would go look for something for Grace, who was proving to be a little difficult.

Jeff watched Holly from a distance as she pulled things off the shelf and studied them thoughtfully. He hadn't realized how much fun shopping for kids was at Christmastime. He fantasized about doing this in the future for his own kids. He looked again at Holly. Boy, was she pretty. He wondered if she could ever be interested in someone like him. Probably not. He dismissed any more foolish thoughts from his head, returning his focus to the lists in his hand.

***

After another hour, Holly, satisfied with what she had chosen for Grace and the arts and crafts kits she'd gathered for Ben, began to make her way over to the part of the store where she had left Jeff. As she rounded the corner, she pulled up short and watched from her position just behind the end of the aisle display. Jeff was riding a mountain bike up and down the aisle. The sight brought a smile to her tired face. By the look on his face, he seemed to be truly enjoying himself and she thought that someday he was going to make a great dad. The thought tugged at her heart. He put the bike back and pulled out a scooter. As he did so, he caught sight of Holly and smiled.

"Hey, I'm going to check out these scooters for Ben."

Before she could answer, he slid off to the opposite end of the aisle. She wheeled her cart toward him. As she did, he turned around and rode toward her. His joyful expression disappeared quickly as the scooter flipped, the front wheel coming off and rolling away in one direction and Jeff tumbling off in the other.

Holly threw her hand to her mouth. Immediately, she was at his side, helping him up.

"Are you hurt?" she asked.

He rubbed his hip. "No, just my pride."

Holly looked at the broken bits of the scooter that now littered the aisle. She smiled. "Well, congratulations. You are now the proud owner of a brand new, broken down scooter!"

***

Holly had gone home and Jeff had unloaded his truck of all the gifts for the Sanders kids and stored them in his garage. He'd drop them off at the firehall in the morning and Mr. and Mrs. Sanders would pick them up from there. He wished he could be there Christmas morning to see the looks on the kids' faces when they opened up their presents. He exited the garage into his kitchen, pressing the button to close the big garage door. He hung his coat in the back hall.

"Come on, Trix, time to go out," he called.

The dog gingerly stepped down from the sofa and walked toward Jeff and the back of the house.

"Just take your time, Trix," he said, then sighed. "You know, if you walked any slower, you'd be going backwards."

He held the back door open for the dog and waited as she trotted out to the fenced-in back yard. His doorbell rang.

Jeff left Trixie out back and went to answer the door, thinking it was most likely Holly. She must have forgotten something. Who else would it be at almost ten o'clock at night?

He was surprised when he found Rosemary standing on his front porch.

"Rosemary! What are you doing here?" Jeff asked. He was slightly irritated. They'd only gone on two dates—he didn't think they were at the point of dropping by each other's houses unannounced.

"I was in the neighborhood and I thought I'd stop in and say hi," she said, smiling. She was decked out in red with a white hat and scarf.

"Well, come on in," he said, opening the door wider. As she followed him in, he turned to her and asked, "How did you know where I lived?"

She gave him a guilty smile. "My bad. I asked Kenny's mom for your address."

Wow, he thought. *She is interested.*

She removed her hat and unwound her scarf, looking around his home. "You've got a nice place here." She sneezed.

"Bless you. Thanks. Would you like coffee? A beer?" he asked.

"Coffee would be great. I hope you don't mind me coming over. I've texted you a few times." She sneezed again.

He wondered if she was sick, and if so, why was she out spreading illness around? "Bless you. I know. I've been busy. Work. We had that big fundraiser for the Sanders family—" Jeff heard the unmistakeable whine of Trixie at the back door. "Hold on a minute, Rosemary."

He went to the back door and let the dog in. She walked past him and headed back to her spot on the sofa.

Rosemary's eyes widened at the sight of the dog. "I didn't know you had a dog."

"That's just Trixie. She's harmless," Jeff said. He noticed blotchy red marks beginning to surface on Rosemary's face. "Hey, are you okay?"

She began digging through her purse. "I'm allergic to dogs."

"You're kidding."

She shook her head. "I wish I was. I need to take an antihistamine. May I have a glass of water?"

"Of course," he said. He went back to the kitchen, took a glass down from the cupboard and filled it with tap water. When he handed it to her, he was alarmed to see her eyes were red, swollen and teary. "You really are allergic."

She sneezed in response. She popped a tablet from a blister pack, put it in her mouth and swallowed, washing it down with a glass of water.

She handed him the empty glass, picked up her coat and put it on. "I'm sorry, Jeff, but I have to go."

Concerned, he said, "Sure, no problem. I understand." He walked her to the door. "Are you sure you're going to be all right?"

She nodded. "Once the antihistamine kicks in." She glanced over at the oblivious Trixie. "And as soon as I leave here."

"Listen, Rosemary, I'm really sorry about this," he said.

She pulled on her gloves. "I'm sure she's a nice dog."

"Are you kidding? Trix is a great dog," he said.

"Listen, Jeff, I have a cousin who has a large farm," she said.

Jeff stared at her. "I'm sorry. I'm not following you."

She laid her hand on his arm. "I mean, if it should work out between us, we'd need to find Trixie a new home." She stepped out onto the porch and wiped her nose with a tissue from her pocket.

Rosemary's automatic assumption that he'd get rid of Trixie annoyed him. He couldn't even look in Trixie's direction. He thought he heard a low whine behind him.

"Listen, Rosemary," he started. There was no easy way to say this. She was a nice girl and he didn't want to hurt her feelings but he wasn't getting rid of his dog. "You seem like a really nice person, but I don't think this is going to work out between us."

"Because of the dog?" she asked, in disbelief.

He looked towards Holly's side of the duplex and said, "There are other reasons as well."

"Thanks for nothing," she said angrily and stomped off his porch, sneezing and wiping her nose.

He felt bad but there was no sense in pursuing it when he was in love with the girl next door. He closed the door behind him. He looked over at his dog and announced, "Don't worry, Trix, you're not going anywhere. We're a package deal, girl."

***

Holly glanced out her bedroom window one last time before climbing into bed, like she did every night, to take a look at all the Christmas lights on the street. She saw a car parked behind Jeff's truck in his driveway. It was a car she hadn't seen before. A blonde woman walked hurriedly down Jeff's driveway toward the car, then got inside and drove away. Who was that?

Holly crawled into bed, tired from the shopping, but in a good way. There was something very pleasurable in buying Santa gifts for children, especially ones who had been through a trauma.

The outing with Jeff had been fun. She lay there, burrowed under the downy blanket with Fernando purring softly beside her, and started to imagine having children of her own, a fantasy that included Jeff. These were dangerous thoughts, she told herself, especially considering the blonde she'd just seen leaving his house. But she decided that just for tonight, as she watched the snow falling lightly outside her bedroom window, she'd allow herself to indulge in the fantasy. She fell asleep with a smile on her face.

***

The next day, Holly told Jeff about her plan to confront Tim.

Jeff rubbed the back of his neck. "I just don't like it, Hol."

"But it has to be done. Needs must and all that."

"Oh, I understand that, but I don't like the idea of you going alone," he said.

"It'll be all right," she protested. She didn't sound convinced to him. Hell, he wasn't convinced.

"He's obviously moved on with his life with the new partner and baby and he may not be real keen on you waltzing in and stirring up the pot," he explained.

He saw a flash of anger behind her eyes. "Well, what am I supposed to do? Just let him get away with it while I continue to pay his half of the debts?" Her eyes blazed with fury, which made them appear greener.

God, she was cute when she was mad, Jeff thought. "No, of course not. My concern is for your welfare and safety. I'd be afraid for you if he became dangerous or something."

She bit her lip. She obviously hadn't thought of that. She could be mad all she wanted to be but he was glad he pointed it out. All that mattered to him was that Holly stayed safe.

In a plea of desperation, he suggested, "Look, I'll wait in the car. Just let me go with you so I know you're safe."

She smiled, stepped toward him and clasped her hands around his. Hers were small and dainty and her touch electrified him. *Geez*, he thought, *she's only touching my hand, how would I handle her touching other parts of me? I'd probably have that heart attack for sure.* Reluctantly and by sheer force of will, he pushed those thoughts out of his mind.

"I really, really appreciate your offer, Jeff," she said softly, looking up at him. "But this is something I have to do for myself. Do you understand?"

He shook his head. "No, I don't."

"It'll be all right. It's broad daylight."

"Okay," he relented, all the while formulating a plan in the back of his mind. "Are you heading out now?"

"Yeah, I think it's best that I go and get it over with," she said.

"Do you want to grab some dinner afterward and you can tell me all about it?"

"I'd love to," she agreed. "I'll call you when I'm leaving there."

"Sounds good."

She left and he watched her out his front window as she pulled out of the driveway and headed down the street.

He grabbed his coat, gloves and keys and locked the door behind him. There was no way in hell he was letting Holly meet this lowlife all by herself, without backup. He just didn't trust the guy. Frankly, he didn't care if she got mad. He wouldn't be able to live with himself if anything happened to her. She could face her ex on her own, but he'd be there in the background. Just in case.

CHAPTER NINETEEN

Holly slowly pulled up in front of the house where she'd last seen Tim. She had not wanted to come until she was prepared. She had gone over and over in her head what she was going to say to him. Since she had no recourse through the courts or the police, she was going to appeal to any shred of decency Tim had left. She was really touched that Jeff had wanted to accompany her. It was comforting to know someone had her back. But despite his chivalrous offer, she didn't want to drag Jeff into the murky waters of her past. She wanted to stand up for herself. She didn't want anyone coming to her rescue. Not even Jeff, as wonderful as he was. She had to do this alone. It was the reason she hadn't told her parents or Emma she had located Tim. In their loyalty, they would have wanted not only to be there with her but to tell Tim what they thought of him, as well, and this just wasn't the time for that. This was the time for Holly and Tim alone.

On the ride over, she'd thought about Tim. Really thought about him—something she hadn't done for real in the two years since he'd disappeared. She had gone through many different phases: disbelief, anger, hurt and sadness. She had worn each phase right into the ground, in fact. But she did not want to end up bitter. She'd fought against that. Sinking into a hole of depression was the trickier problem because it would have been an easy gravitational slide. By the time she'd reached the housing development she'd realized that Tim was in her past. She had no feelings left for him either way. Even so, she wanted justice. And despite everything, she realized she was ready to move on.

She sat in her idling car across the street from the big, beautiful house with the twin wreaths. She wondered whose it was and suspected it belonged to the older couple Holly had seen Tim with the other day. She could only wonder what Tim had told his new family about his past.

She shut the car off, got out and locked the door. She made her way up the paved driveway, freshly cleared with a snowblower by the looks of the neat, straight snowbanks flanking it. She thought two things as she made her way to the front doors of the house. First, that never had a walk up a driveway been so long, and second, that in her panic, she had forgotten her carefully planned speech. Her heart was racing and she felt hot. But her feet kept moving forward and before she knew it, she was standing on the front porch, ringing the doorbell with a shaking hand. *There, I'm committed now,* she thought. She drew in a deep breath as the door opened and she was greeted by the petite woman with the honey blonde hair she'd seen Tim with at the restaurant.

"Can I help you?" The woman smiled, and Holly was aware of the aroma of fresh-baked gingerbread emanating from the house.

In all her preparations and imagined scenarios, Holly had never visualized anyone other than Tim answering the door, which was absurd now that she thought about it. She tried to regroup and forced the words out of her mouth. "Yes. May I speak to Tim?"

The woman frowned, puzzled. "Tim? I'm sorry, but there's no one by that name here. Are you sure you're at the right house?"

Holly nodded but said nothing. She started to second-guess herself. Had she gotten it wrong?

"Have a good evening." The woman started to close the door but Holly held up a hand.

She tried again. "May I speak to your husband?"

The woman hesitated, unsure. Finally, she turned her head and called out, "Jim? Honey, can you come to the door for a minute?" She looked back at Holly as if she were assessing her.

Jim? Maybe Holly had made a mistake. She'd apologize for bothering them and head on her way. But then the husband appeared, with the baby girl in his arms. Up close, Holly saw that it was indeed him. From the mole on his neck to the small chicken pox scar on his forehead, it was definitely Tim, no matter what he was calling himself now.

She looked at the baby, who was no more than five or six months old and was the image of Holly's ex. Holly felt sorry for both the woman and the baby. Like herself, they had not asked for this.

Tim went pale when he saw Holly.

"This woman asked to see you," his wife said.

"Here, Beth, take the baby and go into the other room," Tim said, handing off the child. He did not take his eyes off of Holly.

"What is going on?" Beth demanded.

"It's nothing," he said, pulling his fearful gaze away from Holly long enough to look at his wife. "Give us a minute, will you? I'll take care of this."

The woman looked back and forth between Holly and Tim, uncertain. She hesitated before disappearing into the interior of the house.

Holly started. "Jim? What the hell is going on?"

"Shh, keep your voice down," Tim said. "I can explain everything."

"Can you?" Holly asked, her voice tinged with anger. "How about starting with where you've been the last two years?"

He looked past her, up and down the street, and then over his shoulder. When he spoke, he was practically whispering. "Look, do we really have to do this now? Can I meet you somewhere? Somewhere private?"

"Why? So your wife doesn't hear?" Holly asked. She was by no means going to make it comfortable for him. By the looks of things, he'd been enjoying plenty of comfort.

He sighed heavily.

"She doesn't know, does she?" Holly asked.

He didn't speak. He just shook his head. She'd never realized before how weak he really was. She was well rid of him.

"And whose house is this, anyway?" Holly demanded.

Tim shook his head. He kept his voice down to a near-whisper. "No, she doesn't know. This is her parents' house. We're in town for the holidays, visiting."

"Where are you living now?"

"It doesn't matter where I'm living now."

"It does to me," Holly said bitterly. "Considering I'm still carrying your debt load."

"Look, I don't expect you to understand, but there was no way I was going to be able to rebuild my life with all that hanging over my head," he explained. "I had to start over."

She looked over his shoulder at the front hall with its expensive striped wallpaper and the Persian rug over the black-and-white tiled floor. A majestic grandfather clock stood sentinel in the nook of the staircase. Heavy green garland with big, luxurious red bows wound its way around the banister.

"It must be nice to just skip out on your obligations and press the reset button."

He looked at her sharply and hissed, "I had no choice. I had to reinvent myself. All that debt would have ruined my life."

Holly's eyes blazed with anger. "All that debt did ruin my life! You left me to pay it off!" She was so angry she didn't know whether to scream or throttle him.

The blonde woman had reappeared and stood in the background, but Tim did not appear to notice her.

"What do you want?" he asked Holly coolly.

"What do I want?" she asked, incredulous. "I want you to do the right thing and take responsibility for what you've done. I want you to pay your share."

He made a move to close the door, saying, "Look, this isn't a good time right now."

But Holly wedged her boot in the door. "No, Tim, it is a good time."

Beth spoke from behind her husband. "Jim, why does she keep calling you 'Tim'?"

"Because that's his name," Holly replied. "His real name."

"Look, you need to leave or I'm calling the police," the woman said to Holly, waving Tim aside and taking hold of the door. A flash of something sparkly caught Holly's eye.

"Is that my engagement ring?" Holly asked, furious. "That ring was supposed to be sold to help pay off debts."

Beth looked at the ring on her finger and then at Tim. "Jim, please tell me what's going on," she pleaded.

Holly felt very sorry for the woman. Her world was about to come crashing down.

"What debts?" Beth asked nervously.

"Look, I can explain everything," Tim began.

Holly exploded. "Let me help you, Tim." She noticed the look of panic washing across his face. "Tim and I used to be engaged. We lived together. Well, we did until Tim's gambling problem brought us to ruin. He skipped out about two years ago after we filed for bankruptcy, and left me paying his share of the court-ordered repayment plan as well as my own."

"Two years ago?" Beth repeated. Her expression looked as if she was trying to process what Holly had said, trying to make the math fit. "That was around the time we met."

"Beth, I can explain," he said nervously.

She looked up at him. "Just tell me, Jim. Is what she says true?"

He looked down at the floor. "Some of it," he admitted quietly.

"Some of it?" Holly shouted.

Beth reached out and touched her husband's arm. "Tell me the truth. Some of it? Or all of it?"

He did not lift his gaze up from the ground. "All of it."

"Oh my God," the woman said, leaning back against the front door with a crushed expression on her face. She tried to collect herself. She kept looking back and forth between Tim and Holly, wounded.

Finally, she asked in a shaky voice, "Is your real name James Whitemore?"

He shook his head and said almost inaudibly, "No. It's Timothy Mandelson."

She was speechless, but she took a deep breath and seemed to pull herself together. She staggered over to the hall table and picked up a pen and a notepad. With grim determination on her face, she walked back and handed them to Holly.

"Would you please write down your phone number and email...Holly?"

As Holly scribbled down the information, Beth added, "I will call you, but first I need to process all of this."

"Of course," Holly said, her hand shaking. She handed the notepad back to the woman and their eyes met. Holly knew without a doubt this woman would get in contact with her.

Tim hung his head as Beth closed the front door.

Holly stood there, frozen to the spot, trying to process what had just happened. Her legs were like jelly, but she managed to step off the porch and make her way down the driveway. This wasn't how she'd expected to feel. In all her fantasies, she had ended up feeling triumphant and victorious once she'd found Tim, but now she felt anything but. There was some satisfaction, and there was relief that he had admitted his wrongdoing, but any feelings of victory were non-existent. If anything, she felt a bit hollow. She had just ruined this woman's illusion of a happy life.

When she got to the end of the driveway and began crossing the street to her car, she saw Jeff's truck parked behind hers. She looked up and made eye contact with him and he immediately jumped out of the cab of his truck. She had never been so glad to see anyone. She couldn't speak. Tears rolled down her cheeks. She felt her knees buckle. But Jeff was there and he caught her. "It's all right, Holly. I've got you." He held her tight and she felt safe in his arms. He whispered in her ear, "I'm right here, Hol."

And that was the only good thing in the whole damn day.

CHAPTER TWENTY

Jeff helped Holly up into the passenger side of the truck, then went around to his side and started the engine to get the heater going. He told her not to worry about her car. He'd call Kenny and the two of them could drive back out later to get it.

He reached into his glove box for the package of tissues he kept there and handed it to Holly.

"Do you want to tell me what happened?" he asked.

Holly tearfully relayed the events that had transpired on that front porch.

"Well, that's good, isn't it?" he asked. "He admitted to it. He didn't try to lie his way out of it. And most of all, he didn't hurt you." He could not hide the relief in his voice.

"I should have met him privately. I don't know that woman and I not only just ruined her Christmas but most likely her life, as well," Holly said, looking at Jeff. Her eyes were red-rimmed and her nose was red.

He raised his eyebrows. After all that jerk had put her through, disappearing and leaving her to struggle the last two years, Holly was worried about hurting the woman. Right now, Jeff's immediate concern was Holly.

"Can I tell you how I see it?"

She nodded, not saying anything.

"Yes, you just delivered some really bad news. And yes, she'll probably have a terrible Christmas because of it. But you know what? You did her a favor."

Holly looked at him, frowning. "I hardly think so."

"How long were you with Tim?"

"Almost seven years."

"This woman has been with him two. And obviously, if he's gone and changed his name, he's carried over his honesty issues into this relationship, as well. Yeah, it hurts right now for her, but better now than in seven years, when he's done the same thing to her he did to you."

"I don't know," she said.

"Trust old Jeffie on this one," he assured her.

Despite her distress, Holly managed a smile, which made Jeff feel a little better, too.

"Now, I promised you some dinner once this was over with," he said.

She thought for a moment. "Actually, I am very hungry."

"That's all I need to know," he said.

***

Holly felt numb. She just wanted to go home. Jeff left her to her thoughts for the rest of the drive, and she was grateful to him for leaving her in peace.

"Would you mind if we didn't go out to eat?" she asked. "I prefer to eat in tonight."

"That's fine. I've got a recipe for stir fry that I wanted to try out. What do you say?" he asked.

"Sounds great."

When his truck turned the corner and the duplex came into view, she breathed a sigh of relief. She also felt very tired.

He unlocked the front door to his house and held it open for her. Once inside, she removed her hat and coat and laid them on the back of his sofa. She leaned over and petted Trixie's head. The dog lifted her head and gently nuzzled Holly's hand. *Just like her owner, there's nothing mean about her,* Holly thought.

"Look this will take a few moments, so just sit down with Trix and relax," Jeff suggested.

Holly took him up on his offer. She plopped down on the sofa next to the dog and rested her hand on the dog's back. She listened to the sounds of Jeff preparing dinner: water running, steak sizzling in a pan and the microwave pinging at intervals. Jeff hummed a Christmas tune as he worked in the kitchen. She laid her head back on the sofa and soon the background noise lulled her to sleep.

She woke with Jeff gently shaking her. "Hey, Hol, dinner's ready."

Holly sat up abruptly, momentarily forgetting where she was. She stood up and stretched. Something smelled good. Her stomach growled in response. She followed Jeff to the kitchen and watched as he served steak stir fry, broccoli, and some whole grain rice on dinner plates.

"That looks wonderful," she said.

"I'm learning how to cook for myself. And I'm enjoying it," he said. "I even watched a cooking show on television the other day."

He stood back and the overhead table lamp bathed his face in gold. His was a face she could very easily look at every day for the rest of her life. His warm brown eyes were eyes you could get lost in.

"I'm starving," Holly announced.

"Then you've come to the right place."

The dog, Trixie, practically rolled off the sofa and ambled toward the table, sitting on the floor next to Jeff's chair.

Holly chuckled. "So, she does sit up."

Jeff looked at his dog. "Oh, when it comes to food, Trixie doesn't play."

Holly shook her head and laughed.

Jeff held out his arm, indicating that Holly should sit down. "Did you know that labs have an overeating gene?"

"I did not know that, but thanks for enlightening me," she said. "I'll sleep better having that piece of information tucked safely away in my mind." She looked around at the carefully set table and frowned. "Do you have chopsticks?"

He shook his head. "Uh, do we need them?"

"Hold on, I'll go get some." She smiled when she saw the expression on his face.

"Just for the record, I'm perfectly happy with a fork and a knife," he ventured.

"C'mon, I thought you were going to live life on the edge."

She dashed next door and after rummaging through two kitchen drawers, they were in her grasp. She hadn't used them in a while so she gave them a quick wipe down with the dish towel.

She returned to find Jeff still standing at the table waiting for her. He had put on some Christmas music.

"I've never used chopsticks before," he admitted.

Sitting across the table from him, she smiled. "Don't worry, I'll be gentle."

He grinned in response. She liked how his eyes were full of warmth.

"Again, let me reiterate how happy I am to use a fork and knife," he repeated.

She shook her head. She decided she wasn't going to take no for an answer. He had supported her. Now it was her turn to support him in his desire to try new things. "Come on, Jeff. You'll be able to cross it off your bucket list."

"It's not on my bucket list," he said evenly. "Imagine that."

"Well after tonight, you can add it to your bucket list and then cross it off," she suggested brightly. She handed him a pair of chopsticks.

He looked at her blankly. "That makes no sense."

She raised her eyebrows and shrugged. "It works for me."

"Two sticks? I might as well just use my hands, it might be easier." He scowled at the offending utensils.

Holly held up her hand and demonstrated. "Like this."

She picked up a broccoli floret with her chopsticks. It was delicious and she was so hungry.

She watched as he attempted four times to pick up a piece of steak with increasing frustration.

"Try not to stab the food, it's already dead. Those kamikaze motions won't get you anywhere. Go at it sideways just the way you would with a fork."

"Easy for you to say," he grumbled.

She put her chopsticks down, stood up and moved to the chair next to his. She pulled it up closer to him until the seats of their chairs were touching.

"Let me show you," she suggested. She clasped her hand over his. His skin, though smooth, was hard and slightly darker, whereas her hand was fair and much smaller. She cleared her throat. "The sticks shouldn't be crossed. More like parallel." She entwined her fingers around his, trying to manipulate them into position. Her heartbeat ratcheted up and it felt like all of her five senses were on fire.

"Try to relax. You've got a death grip on them." She laughed. She began to rub his knuckles and felt his hand loosen up. She slid the chopsticks out of his hand.

She handed him the first one and said, "Hold this like a pencil. Now slide the other one in between your fingers."

He turned his head toward her and whispered, "Like this?"

She could feel his warm breath on her cheek and she was aware of his scent: a pleasant mixture of aftershave, laundry detergent, and mint. His face was mere inches from hers. She refused to look at him. It felt like the ground was shifting beneath her. Suddenly, she felt his fingers underneath her chin, turning her face toward him. She swallowed hard. Very gently, as if she might break, he placed his hand on her face and laid the sweetest kiss on her lips. She closed her eyes and relished the warmth and firmness of his lips. It had been a long time since she'd been kissed.

"Hol," he whispered. He kissed her again, hesitantly at first, but then with insistence.

What am I doing? she thought to herself. Abruptly, although not without regret, she pulled away from him. She stood up so quickly, she knocked the chair over. The dog, who had resigned herself to lying under the table, jumped up and barked.

"I'm sorry, Jeff," Holly said. What made everything worse was the wounded look on Jeff's face as she bolted from his home.

CHAPTER TWENTY-ONE

While Holly was working her shift at the restaurant on Christmas Eve, Jeff unlocked the garage door on her side of the duplex. He looked around grimly. He had hoped there'd be some boxes marked 'Christmas' but there was not one. The garage was bare. There was only her wheelie bin for garbage. There were no tools, no garden equipment. He'd been aghast when he realized she was serious about not putting up any Christmas decorations. But it was because she didn't have any and she was too broke to buy them. He knew she was struggling with all that had happened but it was important not to give up. He had rung her parents, her sister, his mother and Stan across the street and told them he needed help with a very important mission regarding Holly. They all agreed to meet at his house at noon. Holly wasn't expected home until four after the extra shift she'd picked up at the restaurant. Everything would be done by then.

He had had this brainchild last night after he'd kissed her. He hadn't seen her since and he was going to give her all the space she needed. But he had decided that this was going to be his way of apologizing to her. Jeff had wanted to kick himself after that disaster. What on earth had possessed him to kiss her like that? Especially after the day she'd had. His timing couldn't have been worse. If there were prizes being giving out for stupidity, Jeff Kowalek would sweep them. He couldn't help the way he felt about her, though. It would be a dream come true if she felt the same way about him. But her running out on him wasn't a good sign. As for himself, he knew one thing: Holly Fulbright was the only one for him.

He locked the door behind him and looked at his watch. He had to get a move on. He had one errand to run before they all got there.

***

Jeff backed into his driveway, trying to see over the fresh cut Christmas tree in the bed of his truck. He saw Holly's parents standing on his side of the porch. From the bags in their hands, he could see they had come prepared with Christmas decorations. He hoped they hadn't been waiting long.

He parked the truck and jumped out.

"Hey, Mr. and Mrs. Fulbright, thanks so much for coming," Jeff said.

"We've been waiting out here for ten minutes," Mr. Fulbright said gruffly. "Do you know it's freezing out here?"

Gloria elbowed him. "Give him a chance, Alan."

"I'm so sorry Mr. and Mrs. Fulbright, there was an accident and traffic was backed up," he explained. He hoped Mr. Fulbright's salty mood would improve.

He walked over to Holly's side of the duplex and pulled out his keys again. "Well, this is a surprise for Holly."

"We didn't say anything," Gloria said. "I think it's a fantastic idea."

Hand on the doorknob, he turned to Holly's parents and said, "It comes as no shock to anyone that Holly is struggling financially. I thought we could all chip in and decorate her place for her."

"I have to admit it is a good idea in the spirit of things," Alan conceded. "Holly loves Christmas. Both my girls always loved Christmas. When she lived at home, you had to keep moving or you'd end up decorated yourself."

The door popped open and they followed Jeff inside. Daylight cast the apartment in a faded light. Looking around at the beige carpet, the minimal furniture and the general lack of things, it was impossible to tell it was the day before Christmas.

Gloria looked around and said, "We've got a lot of work to do."

"Why didn't she ask me? I'd give her the money to buy some decorations," her father said, not understanding.

"She's too proud," her mother said simply, looking around her daughter's home. "She won't take our help for her debts but we will get her place decorated properly for Christmas."

Alan Fulbright had a grim look on his face and said quietly, "Agreed."

There was a knock on the door and Jeff opened it to his mother and Morty. He looked beyond them to see Holly's sister, Emma, coming up the driveway with her Sarah and Emily.

"Here we are Jeff," Ginger said. "I've picked up some goodies so we can nibble on them while we work." She had a sandwich tray and a platter of cookies.

"How's work?" Morty asked, chomping on his cigar. He carried two liters of soda and a bag of ornaments.

"The usual, trying not to get burned out," Jeff said.

Morty laughed. "That's a good one, I get it."

Jeff had asked everyone to just bring one box or bag of tree ornaments and one other decoration. Everybody arrived in good time and got right into the swing of things. There was a buzz of excited chatter as everyone took to the task. Even Alan Fulbright did what was asked, offering no blustery comment. Emma parked her two daughters at the kitchen table with paper and magic markers and the instructions to make some Christmas drawings for Aunt Holly's fridge.

Stan and Gladys arrived.

"Thank you so much for coming," Jeff said. He invited them in.

"We've brought the most important thing," Gladys said. She held up a ball of mistletoe.

"Okay, then," Jeff said.

Jeff eventually hauled the tree in and put his hands on his hips. "Damn. I forgot to pick up a tree stand."

"And we have no lights for the tree," Emma said, sorting through the boxes of ornaments that had gathered on the floor.

"I'll go up to Home Depot and get a tree stand and lights," Alan Fulbright said, reaching for his coat. "Do we need anything else? Make a list for me."

"Just get back before Holly gets home," Gloria said.

"I'm well aware of the remit, Gloria," Alan said sternly.

"Grandma, when can we hang the ornaments on the tree?" Sarah asked, at Gloria's elbow.

"As soon as the lights go up," she answered.

***

Holly said goodnight to the girls coming on for the dinner shift, wishing them all a Merry Christmas. She was officially off until after the holiday. It was nearing five and she no longer had an excuse to stay at work. Sylvia had handed her a Christmas tin full of baklava and pressed an envelope into her hand. And when Holly looked inside, she saw some cash and tears filled her eyes. Sylvia hugged her and said "Don't fuss now. Ted and I give all our employees a tin of baklava and a little bonus. Merry Christmas, dear." It may have not seemed like much to Sylvia but to Holly, it was a lot. In her mind, she was already thinking about what she'd get with that bonus. Impulsively, she threw her arms around Sylvia's neck again, catching her by surprise. "Have the best Christmas ever, Sylvia!"

Walking to her car, she sighed. She was feeling slightly better than she had at the beginning of the month. Suddenly, she felt a wave of melancholia and nostalgia all at once. She sighed, feeling unable to move. She remembered Christmases as a kid. How she'd loved them. Even after she was older, and no longer believed in Santa Claus, she'd still believed in the magic of Christmas. As teenagers, she and Emma would set their alarms for six in the morning, much to their father's chagrin. The joy of descending the staircase to find all the presents under the lit-up Christmas tree—she was determined to feel that way again.

She was expected to join her parents at her sister's Christmas morning for brunch and then back to her house for dinner. It was always a full-on day. She was beginning to look forward to it. She walked to the parking lot behind the restaurant. Snow fell lightly. It was quiet outside. There was a sense of peace in the air. She warmed up her car and headed home.

***

She thought about Jeff on the ride home. In fact, Jeff had dominated her thoughts since he'd kissed her last night. There had been joy and magic in that kiss. She sighed, thinking about it. She regretted rushing out on him. He'd think she wasn't interested and nothing could be farther from the truth.

Thirty minutes after she left work, she made a left on a secondary street and then after about one hundred yards, she turned right onto the street where she lived. She was thinking about what TV show she would binge watch that evening, trying to decide what she was in the mood for. Maybe crime drama. Or horror. Or maybe even something Christmassy. She gave it some thought. Something at her house caught her eye. She braked gently as she approached it. There were Christmas lights hanging up outside. They were those icicle lights she had always liked and they hung off her gutter like a curtain and wound all the way around the second story of the house. She looked up in amazement. She noticed her parents' car parked in her driveway as well as her sister's car out front. She wondered what they were up to. She suspected Jeff had hung the lights. Why not? He'd done it for all the other neighbors on the street. Anxiety took hold of her. With great trepidation, she walked up the driveway. As she stepped up onto the porch, she could hear their voices inside. A Christmas party at her house and she wasn't even there.

She turned the doorknob gently and the door slowly opened. She stepped into her living room quietly. She took it all in: the lights, the decorations, the smell of cinnamon and cloves and fresh baked goods. She looked around. Her father was laughing with Ginger in front of the tree. The tree! The top of it touched the ceiling. Jeff stood on a ladder, trying to get the star on the top branch. Christmas music played in the background and one of her nieces flew by, chased by the other.

Holly felt her eyes fill with tears. It looked magical. She put her hands to her mouth.

"Holly!" her mother exclaimed.

Everyone stopped what they were doing and turned to her, and then in a wave of voices chorused, "Merry Christmas!"

And then it came—a great tidal wave of feeling that threatened to sweep Holly away. Because deep down, she really wanted to celebrate Christmas. But it was so buried under layers and layers of misfortune that it took her family and friends to help pull her out from underneath all of that.

Everybody went quiet. Holly tried to quell her sobs but she couldn't suppress them. She didn't miss the odd expression on her father's face. She saw the sympathy on Ginger's face and when she looked up at Jeff on the ladder, she saw that his face was full of tenderness and something else. Her sister and mother immediately rushed toward her, but her father held them back, stopping them, his arm across them like a bar. He came to her and she looked at him in confusion, unsure. Her father didn't do hugs and affection. He hesitated just a bit when he reached her and she whispered, "Dad?"

He pulled her into his embrace and hugged her, speaking quietly into her ear. "Honey, everything is going to be all right." Holly clung to her father and cried.

***

Holly bundled up in her coat, scarf, and hat and stepped outside into the brisk, cold night. Stars littered the dark sky. She drew in a breath of cold, crisp air. The houses on the street were lit up in various colors and now hers was one of them.

She closed the door behind her, needing a few moments to pull herself together. She was so touched by all of their combined efforts and for the first time in a very long time, she felt loved.

The front door opened and Jeff stepped tentatively out onto the porch. "Hol? You okay?"

She nodded without speaking; she didn't trust her voice. He was the only one who had ever called her 'Hol.' Even Tim had always called her 'Holly.' That abbreviation of her name, used by him and no other, felt intimate. And she liked it.

Jeff's voice came out nervous and rushed. "Look, if I've crossed a boundary, let me know. I can take it all down and send everyone home."

She shook her head. Without speaking, she reached out and touched his arm. She nodded toward the house. Finally, she found her voice. "I think it's absolutely wonderful." She felt the tension leave his body. She did not remove her hand from his arm and he didn't pull away.

"Thank you," she whispered.

"It was my way of apologizing for kissing you." He looked at the ground.

She had something else to say, as well. There were no secrets between them but she needed to put this out there. "Do you realize how much baggage I come with?"

"I am aware," he said quietly. But then he broke into a grin. "But you're not the only one with baggage. Mine comes with its own luggage rack!"

"It's not funny," she protested half-heartedly. Despite herself, she laughed.

He nodded his head. "Yeah, it is. Because it has to be. It may help you get through it if you can have a laugh over it."

"What about the blonde?" She withdrew her arm from his.

"What blonde?" he repeated.

"The one I saw leaving your house the other night."

"Oh! You mean Rosemary? She's nothing to worry about," he explained. "We went out a couple of times but she's not for me."

Holly raised her eyebrows.

"No, seriously," he said. "Besides, she's allergic to dogs and before I knew it, she was trying to foster Trixie out to some relative with a farm." He laughed, shaking his head.

"Oh no, poor Trixie."

"And how can I go out with anyone else when I'm—"

The front door opened and Holly's father stepped out onto the porch. He cleared his throat.

"I'll head back inside," Jeff said quietly. He disappeared into the house.

Alan Fulbright leaned against the porch railing.

"Thanks for the lights, Dad, I appreciate it," she said quietly. She stood next to him.

"You're welcome," he said. He didn't add anything and Holly felt the awkward silence grow between them. It was a little sad. Here she was, alone with her father, and neither one had anything to say to the other. The very idea threatened to cast a pall over the whole, beautiful evening.

Her father started speaking, his voice so low and soft she almost missed it.

"My father was a Marine," he said.

She didn't know much about her grandfather, who'd died before she was born, but she'd known this one fact. Her father almost never spoke about him.

"He ran our home like a barracks," Alan said. From his tone, Holly guessed it hadn't been pleasant.

Her dad continued. "My father was an excellent Marine. But he was a lousy father."

Holly's eyes widened in surprise.

Her father turned to her and she saw the sadness contorting his features. "There was no crying in our house. There was also no affection. You took things like a man. Even if you were only six years old."

Holly didn't say anything. She didn't know what to say.

"When I married your mother, I promised myself I would be a different father than my own was."

Holly looked away, uncomfortable.

"You've had a terrible couple of years. And I wanted to help, but I don't know how. The only way I know how to help people is to give them money." He grimaced as he said it.

Holly lowered her head and whispered, "I'm sorry, Dad."

Her father gave a brittle laugh. "You've nothing to be sorry about. I'm the one who's sorry."

They were both quiet for a moment and Holly leaned her head against the upright railing.

"I didn't want to be like him and yet I've turned out just like him."

Holly said nothing. It wouldn't be right to protest or try to convince him otherwise, it would have been an outright lie and both of them would have known it. He spoke the truth: he hadn't been the greatest of fathers. Still, she supposed it was something that at least he acknowledged it. Maybe he only needed a nudge in the right direction.

"Dad, sometimes, it's just enough to listen," she said.

He looked at her. "I don't even know how to do that without a sarcastic comment."

"It's not too late to try," she said softly.

He smiled at her.

Holly felt something she hadn't felt in a long time. Hope.

***

It was late when everyone finally left. Holly was finally alone with Jeff. She held a purring Fernando in her arms.

"Jeff, I need to say something to you," she started. She wanted to finish what she'd meant to say before her father had cut their conversation short earlier.

His ringing cell phone interrupted her. He glanced at it and frowned. "Hold on, Hol, I have to take this." He answered it and the exchange was brief.

"I have to go into work," he said quietly. All traces of laughter had left his face.

"But it's Christmas Eve," Holly pointed out.

"They're calling in everyone, all off duty firefighters," he explained.

Holly felt something in her chest tighten. "Where is it?"

"It's that old industrial complex out on Route 261," he said. He picked up his jacket and headed toward the door. "I've got to go."

"Oh no," Holly said, following him out, clutching her cat.

On the porch, he turned around and asked, "Can I ask you to take Trixie out and give her some dinner? The chow is in the back hall."

She nodded. "No problem. I'll take care of her while you're gone."

"Thanks, Hol. Do you know where I keep the spare key?" he asked, lowering his voice.

"I do."

Worried, she reached out and touched his arm. "Jeff, be careful."

He grinned. "No worries, Hol."

He paused and turned back to her. "Look, Holly, I want to apologize again for last night. For kissing you. The last thing I want to do is turn into one of those landlords—"

"There's nothing to apologize for." She gave him a reassuring smile. Suddenly, she felt very worried about him. "Can we talk when you come home?"

"I'd like that," he said quietly.

She waited until his truck disappeared down the road before returning inside. The cat jumped down as soon as she closed the door and

Holly felt her insides grow heavy as she waited for Jeff to come back home.

CHAPTER TWENTY-TWO

In his eight years as a firefighter, Jeff had only been called in two other times to a four- and five-alarm fire. Each time had been difficult, scary and exhilarating.

He headed toward the firehouse and as he pulled his truck into the back lot, the garage doors on the back of the firehouse were open. He trotted into the house and pulled his gear on quickly. There were two trucks getting ready to roll out and from the first one, someone yelled: "Come on Kowalek, get in. We've got room for one more." He hopped into the back seat of the truck. Once he did, the truck rolled out of the garage.

As soon as they turned onto Route 261, Jeff saw a great plume of black smoke billowing upwards, despite the night sky. The snow fell lightly.

Fire engines were double parked along the curb, their lights flashing and their sirens screaming. There had to be at least two hundred fire-fighters around the place. Two and three inch diameter hoses coursed from the pumpers and hydrants into the burning building.

He caught sight of Kenny, whose face was blackened with smoke.

"Where's the incident commander?" Jeff asked.

Kenny coughed and said: "Over by pumper one."

"Ok, thanks," Jeff said, slapping him on the back. Kenny took off in another direction. There was no time for chat. He broke into a trot until he found the incident commander.

"Kowalek," was all the man said in acknowledgement.

"It looks like everyone and his brother is here," Jeff observed.

The chief nodded. "It's now a five alarm. We've requested back up from neighboring towns and any volunteers." The commanding officer looked around. "Go assist with the ladder trucks, Jeff. I'm pulling everyone out of the building."

He headed toward the ladder trucks, which were getting into position. The use of ladder trucks was not a good sign. Most fires were fought from the interior of a building. Ladder trucks were used when the fire became out of control and it had to be fought from the exterior. As if on cue, the firemen who had been inside fighting the fire, poured out of the burning building, dragging the hoses out with them.

Jeff immediately went to work, accepting the fact that he was in for a long night.

**

Holly stood at her front window, framed by twinkling, multi-colored lights, and watched the snow falling heavily. She had watched the local news and their coverage of the massive fire at the industrial complex. The footage showed huge plumes of bright orange flames illuminating the night sky. Thinking of Jeff, she swallowed hard. Why was it that everything seemed worse at night? She'd found that on the nights he worked, the duplex felt different. She didn't like the feeling. She felt lonely. She liked knowing he was right next door if she needed anything. She would run over at eleven and take Trixie out—that's if she could get her out—and make sure she had enough water in her bowl. She might even try to coax her over to her place.

Her sister had given her ready-made packets of mulled wine mix. All she had to do was add a bottle of wine and boil it on the stove. She could manage that. She added one clove and a couple slices of orange. The house was quiet. She supposed she could play Christmas music but was too restless as she waited for Jeff to come home. She could watch TV but she wasn't in the mood for that, either. With a glass of warm, mulled wine in hand, she kept walking to her front window to check to see if Jeff's truck had returned yet. She grew more worried every time it hadn't. She thought about their kiss. Foolishly, she had run away from it, scared of a possible new relationship. And very afraid of repeating the mistakes of the past. But it had been two years since she and Tim went their separate ways. It wasn't like it had just happened last week. Jeff was so kind, always helping everyone out. And he was funny. She had never met anyone who made her laugh as hard as he did. She shook her head and smiled to herself. She sipped her wine and watched from the window, Christmas lights blinking, waiting for Jeff to come home. The thing was, she was ready to move on from her past. And she wanted to move on with Jeff Kowalek.

***

Holly woke when she heard Jeff's truck pull into his driveway next door. She rubbed her eyes and looked at the clock. It was going for five in the morning. She peered through the blinds and saw him getting out and digging through his gear in the back.

She took her robe off the chair and slipped it on, pulling the sash tight around her. She flew down the stairs and out her front door, not caring that she had no coat on. Because some things were so important they just couldn't wait.

"Jeff?"

He was at his front door, surprised to see her so early in the morning. It was still dark out.

"Hol? Is everything all right?" he asked with alarm on his face. He opened the door and waited for her to enter first. "Come in."

In the light of the room, she noticed how fatigued he looked. His face was covered in sweat and black soot.

She approached him and with great tenderness and care, she took his face in her hands, noting his look of pleasant surprise.

"Do not ever apologize for kissing me again," she said, and she leaned in and kissed him softly and warmly on the lips, revelling when she felt his strong arms sliding around her waist.

Jeff looked at her and said softly, "Merry Christmas, Hol."

EPILOGUE

December 2018

"Hey, Holly, the new tenant is here," Jeff called from the kitchen. "At least, I think it's them," he said, peering through the blinds.

Holly padded down the stairs, dressed casually in jeans and a turtleneck and cardigan. She came up behind Jeff, wrapped her arms around his waist and laid her head on his back.

"Good morning," she purred.

"Good morning to you, too," he said, smiling. He glanced down at the gold wedding band on his ring finger. He still couldn't believe his luck. How things had changed since last year. After his cardiac event, he'd had enough of a scare to make him sit up and take an honest look at his life. He'd realized he didn't want to continue the path he was on. He'd started walking up and down the street, and it had been difficult at first because he was so out of shape. But he'd persisted and now was down twenty pounds and walking five miles, five times a week. He was even taking Trixie along. She always resisted, but once she got going she seemed to enjoy it. If someone had told him a year ago that he and his dog would be physically active, he would never have believed it. He'd also expanded his cooking repertoire, graduating beyond salads and falling in love with grilling. There were now five to six meals that were part of his core group. He turned around, slipping an arm around Holly's shoulders. Trixie ran by, being chased by Fernando.

"Hey, no running in the house, you two," he yelled. "Never thought I'd hear myself telling Trixie to calm down." He laughed. It turned out all Trixie had needed was a friend. And Fernando had fit the bill.

But the biggest change had been Holly. He looked at her and still couldn't believe they were married. They'd arranged for the ceremony to take place at the beginning of the month because they had both agreed that Christmastime was their favorite time of year.

"There's coffee there in the pot," Jeff said to Holly.

She shook her head. "I'll wait until I get to the diner."

Jeff nodded and smiled. She grabbed the car keys off the counter and headed for the door.

"What time are Kenny and Tina meeting us?" she asked, her hand on the doorknob.

"I told them to be here no later than noon. It's an hour's drive to Wilson's Christmas Tree Farm."

"You've got everything we need to cut down a tree?" she asked.

He smiled. "The only job you have, Hol, is to pick one out. I'll get it down for you."

Jeff rinsed out his coffee mug, whistled a Christmas tune and headed out the front door to see if the new tenant needed any help.

***

Holly drove down the street, cautious of the packed snow on the road. Previous cars had made a path for her but still, she didn't want to end up in a ditch. The diner was only ten minutes from their home. She looked happily at the sparkly diamond wedding set on her finger, unable to believe how much things had turned around for her. She was still paying off her debt, but she had another year under her belt. Three down, two to go. And Beth had indeed been in touch, and Tim was now paying his portion. Beth had told Holly she had given him an ultimatum: either do the right thing and pay off his debts or she'd take their daughter and leave him. He had also repaid his share from the first two years he'd skipped out on. Because of this, Holly had been able to quit her job at the Olympic. She and Jeff stopped in from time to time so she could see Sylvia, Ted and the rest of the staff.

As she pulled into the diner near her home, she spotted her father in the rearview mirror, pulling in behind her. She gave him a wave and a smile. At her mother's encouragement, Holly and her Dad met up every Saturday morning for breakfast. They'd started doing this back in the spring. At first, it had been awkward but they'd soldiered on, determined to spend time with each other. Now it was better, and that alone was nothing short of miraculous. They talked about everything and anything and nothing at all. Her father couldn't change who he was; he hadn't hugged her since last Christmas Eve and Holly was perfectly okay with that. For right now, their Saturday morning breakfast was enough.

Her father pulled his car next to hers. He stepped out and signaled for her to come over.

"Good morning, Holly," he said gruffly.

"Hi, Dad."

He glanced around the parking lot, making sure no one was in view or earshot. He handed her some pamphlets and a business card. The way he was acting you'd think a drug deal was about to go down.

"Last week, you mentioned about wanting to start over. And although things are tight, you can start with a small amount. Say twenty-five dollars a week," he said.

Holly leafed through the brochures. They covered various topics on savings and investing. Her dad had listened to her last week about how she wanted to start saving again but could only afford to do a little bit. She wanted to be in control of her own financial destiny.

"It's a start. And everyone has to start somewhere," he said. "You can increase it as your financial situation improves."

"Thanks, Dad."

"I stopped in to see my broker and he gave me these as a starting point," he explained.

Holly was touched that her dad had gone to all this trouble during the week.

"I will definitely look these over."

Her father tapped the front of the business card in her hand. "That's my broker. If you want to go and talk to him. No pressure."

Holly hesitated. "But I don't have any money to invest. Like you said, I would be starting off small."

Alan Fulbright shook his head. "This man isn't just about investing your money. He's all about building relationships."

"Okay, Dad, thanks again," she said.

"Just something to think about," he said.

She tucked the pamphlets into her purse and gave him a bright smile. "Are you hungry?"

"Starved. Your mother was shooing me out of the house so she could get started on her Christmas baking."

They made their way through the slushy parking lot and Holly couldn't ever remember feeling as content as she did at that moment.

"How's Jeff?"

"He's good. We're going out this afternoon to get a Christmas tree."

Her father nodded. He held open the door of the diner for Holly. She was blasted with warm air and the smell of freshly brewed coffee. A faint Christmas song could be heard above the din of the conversations.

"Some wonderful things happen at Christmas," her dad remarked.

"They sure do," she agreed.

***

To receive exclusive bonus material and stay up to date with new releases, you can sign up for my newsletter at www.michelebrouder.com

Also By Michele Brouder

The Happy Holidays Series
A Whyte Christmas
This Christmas
A Wish for Christmas
One Kiss for Christmas
A Wedding for Christmas

***

Escape to Ireland Series
A Match Made in Ireland
Her Fake Irish Husband
Her Irish Inheritance
A Match for the Matchmaker
Home, Sweet Irish Home
An Irish Christmas

ACKNOWLEDGEMENTS

This Christmas

There are always many people involved in the production of a book from its inception to its publication. Book publishing is definitely not a one-man show.

My gratitude to those who assisted with the writing of this book:

Jessica Peirce, my editor, who always has the right answers to all my questions.

Matt Giacomini, Chief of Lakeshore Volunteer Fire Department; Henry Zimmer, Lackawanna Fire Department, Retired; Jennifer Skowronski, RN, Visiting Nurses Association, and Michael Barrett from Cole, Sorrentino, Hurley, Hewner & Gambino, P.C. for assistance with various details. Any mistakes are solely mine.

Patty Gordon for graciously sparing some time to do a read through of the first draft. Thank-you.

CPSIA information can be obtained
at www.ICGtesting.com
Printed in the USA
BVHW070813151121
621680BV00006B/339